"I'm not leavi *your back pocket,"* **Clay said.**

"Why? What we had is over, Clay. History."

"I've been without you for over a year, Nicole. Never again." He moved to block her escape from him, taking her hands in his and pulling her to him. No other woman felt like Nicole, was as feminine or desirable as Nicole. There was no one else for him but her, and there never would be.

"Let me go, Clay. I don't want this. I don't want you," Nicole insisted.

He began covering her throat with tiny kisses, tightening his hold on her, and Nicole felt her body betray her.

"You do want me, Nicole. I've already convinced your body. Now I have to convince your pride."

"My pride was all I had left when you vanished from my life. I won't give you that too . . ."

WHAT ARE *LOVESWEPT* ROMANCES?

They are stories of true romance and touching emotion. We believe those two very important ingredients are constants in our highly sensual and very believable stories in the *LOVESWEPT* line. Our goal is to give you, the reader, stories of consistently high quality that may sometimes make you laugh, sometimes make you cry, but are always fresh and creative and contain many delightful surprises within their pages.

Most romance fans read an enormous number of books. Those they truly love, they keep. Others may be traded with friends and soon forgotten. We hope that each *LOVESWEPT* romance will be a treasure—a "keeper." We will always try to publish

LOVE STORIES YOU'LL NEVER FORGET
BY AUTHORS YOU'LL ALWAYS REMEMBER

The Editors

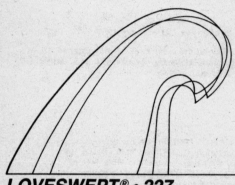

LOVESWEPT® • 227

Patt Bucheister
Two Roads

 BANTAM BOOKS
TORONTO • NEW YORK • LONDON • SYDNEY • AUCKLAND

TWO ROADS

A Bantam Book / December 1987

*If you would be interested in receiving protective vinyl
covers for your Loveswept books, please write to this address
for information:*

Loveswept
Bantam Books
P.O. Box 985
Hicksville, NY 11802

ISBN 0-553-21864-6

Published simultaneously in the United States and Canada

PRINTED IN THE UNITED STATES OF AMERICA

O   0 9 8 7 6 5 4 3 2 1

One

For the first time in thirty-two years, Clay McMasters thought he was going to faint.

The room seemed to spin and he leaned against a table for support. His fingers gripped the frame of the painting he had just purchased, his knuckles white.

The last time he had seen this painting, it had been hanging on the living room wall of Nicole Piccolo's apartment over a year and a half ago. When he had seen it on display in the window of the art gallery, he had known he had to have it. He didn't know how it had gotten there, only that he wanted it—even though it brought back painful memories of the silver-haired woman who had painted it. Her painting would be all he would have of the woman who had filled his soul with delirious joy and his body with the sweet agony of desire, the woman who he thought had died in a car accident over a year ago.

Now the director of the art gallery said Nicole was very much alive!

The director was staring at Clay with concern, obviously alarmed at the shocked expression Clay knew was on his face. "Can I get you a glass of water, Mr. McMasters?" the director asked. "Perhaps you had better sit down."

Clay dismissed the director's suggestion with a shake of his head. He didn't need water or a chair. He needed answers.

The director went to the water cooler anyway and filled a paper cup with water. Clay's hand was trembling slightly as he took the cup. "Are you sure you're all right, Mr. McMasters? You look like you've seen a ghost."

A harsh sound erupted from Clay. "I just heard about one." He took a deep, steadying breath. "Repeat what you said about Nicole Piccolo."

"I have one other painting done by Miss Piccolo in the gallery if you would like to see it. She's going to have an exhibit here in November. Since you appear to like this painting, I thought you might want to see more of her work. It will be her first big exhibit in San Francisco and we think she will sell every painting as soon as the public sees her unique style."

"Are you sure the artist is Nicole Piccolo? A woman with silvery-blond hair and gray eyes, about five feet five?" And satiny skin to drive a man mad, Clay added silently. A small, delicate woman with slim hips and firm breasts, and a husky laugh that had never failed to stir him. A woman he thought was dead.

"I'm quite sure, Mr. McMasters," the director

said with an edge of frost in his voice, apparently not appreciating the implication that he didn't know what he was talking about. "Miss Piccolo and I finalized the arrangements for the exhibit this morning."

"She was here?"

"Yes. She left about an hour ago."

Clay cursed at fate under his breath. If he had been here an hour ago, he could have seen her, talked to her, touched her. If he had walked by the gallery before lunch instead of after, he might have seen her! His mind reeled. Nicole was alive. He still found it hard to believe, but he wanted to believe it more than anything. He had to see her, to touch her. She had to be alive.

Where was she now? He felt as though his blood were just beginning to flow through his veins again after lying stagnant for so long. The shock was beginning to wear off and hope was taking its place. "Did she happen to say where she was going when she left?"

"No. She didn't. Nor did I ask."

"I need her address. It's important that I find her."

"I'm sorry, Mr. McMasters. I can't give out any of our artists' addresses. We have to respect their privacy. If you wish to leave a message, I'll see that Miss Piccolo gets it."

What kind of message could he leave? Clay wondered. Perhaps she thought he had died in the car accident too. His mind raced back to the day he had woken up in the hospital and heard his father tell him the woman with him in the car had died. He hadn't questioned his father. The details hadn't mattered. Nothing had seemed important after hearing the devastating news that Nicole was dead.

What had Nicole been told after the accident? She hadn't come to his room in the hospital or tried to get in touch with him. Would it be a shock to her to discover he was alive when she thought he had died? What in hell had happened after the accident?

Someone knew the answers to those questions. His father.

The director was waiting for some sort of reply. Clay gave him one. "There's no message, but I would like to buy that other painting you mentioned."

The director gladly took Clay's money for both paintings and even wrapped them himself in heavy brown paper. As he walked to his car carrying the paintings, Clay decided he would talk to his father first. Then he would find Nicole.

He drove toward the McMasters Building and, keeping his eyes on the heavy downtown traffic, reached for the phone attached to the console between the two front seats. With his thumb he punched out a phone number.

A minute later he was talking to his partner, who immediately reminded him of the meeting scheduled in fifteen minutes.

"Tell me you're in the parking lot, Clay, and that you'll be up here in a flash."

"Sorry, Darrell. I can't make the meeting. In fact, I doubt if I'll make it back to the office at all today."

Darrell Bowers was noted for his calm reaction

to any problem, big or small. Rarely did he lose his temper or even raise his voice. Knowing Clay would miss the meeting with Carothers, Inc., only under extreme circumstances, Darrell didn't argue the point, although he felt justified in asking, "What's up?"

"Nicole is alive."

There was a choking sound on the other end of the phone. "How? Ah, I mean, are you sure?"

"Enough to try to find her. That's why I won't be coming back to the office today, maybe even for a couple of days. It depends on how long it takes me to find her. The figures I've worked up for the meeting are in a file marked 'Carothers' on my desk. I know I'm dumping all the work on you, Darrell, but I have to do this."

"Don't worry about a thing here. Just keep in touch."

Clay said he would and hung up the phone, shifting his mind away from work to concentrate on the little chat he planned to have with his father.

It took a while to find a parking space, but eventually he was riding the elevator to the top floor of the McMasters Building. The first obstacle was his father's stern secretary, who emphatically told Clay that Mr. McMasters was in a board meeting and absolutely, positively could not be disturbed. Her high-handed manner usually worked to discourage debate in any form, and, confident her words would be taken as law, she turned her attention back to the work on her desk—which was why she didn't see Clay go in the direction opposite to the one he should have taken.

The next obstacle was finding which of the many doors in the office complex led to the room where the board meeting was being held. Clay rarely came to see his father, so he wasn't too familiar with the general layout. He just kept opening doors until he found the right one.

Hugh McMasters was obviously not pleased when Clay stepped into the conference room. The glowering look he bestowed on his son failed to have any effect, however, nor did a stern command for Clay to wait in his office.

Ignoring the other six men sitting on either side of the table, Clay said, "I want to talk to you." After a short pause, he added, "Now."

"I'm busy, as you can see, Clayton. I'll be through in an hour or so." Returning his attention to the portfolio on the polished table in front of him, he spoke to the man on his left. "You were about to quote the figures for the—"

"*Now!*"

Several of the men jumped in their seats as Clay's raised voice pierced the air.

His father's face became flushed with rage. Standing up, he tugged at the bottom of the vest he wore under his dark gray custom-made suit. With deliberate steps meant to intimidate, Hugh walked toward his son, stopping a foot away from him.

Clay had often been told how much he resembled his father. Like his father, he was tall, and both of them had raven-black hair, although there were flecks of distinguished-looking gray throughout his father's thick, styled hair. The high cheekbones and aquiline noses were similar in shape, but their eyes were different, not so much in color as in expression. Clay knew his dark eyes were not as hard and cold as his father's.

"Go to my office, Clayton," Hugh said in a low, firm voice.

Opening the door wider, Clay gestured with a sweep of his hand. "After you."

His father ignored the open doorway. "Do I need to call Security to have you forcibly removed?"

Crossing his arms over his chest, Clay gave his father a faint smile. "If you wish."

After staring at Clay for a long moment, Hugh turned to address the board members. "Gentlemen, excuse me for a few minutes."

Clay followed his father, noting the rigid set to his shoulders. For about the hundredth time, he wished things were different between him and his father, but he knew they never would be. A long time ago he had learned his father's priorities were business, money, and prestige. His family came way down the list.

Clay smiled pleasantly at his father's secretary as he passed her desk on his way into his father's private office. His smile wasn't returned.

By the time Clay had shut the door, Hugh was sitting behind his large cherry desk. Clay discreetly locked the door.

"You had better have a damn good explanation for your behavior, Clayton," Hugh said icily.

"I do." Sitting in one of the dark red leather chairs facing the desk, Clay carefully watched his father's expression. "Nicole Piccolo."

Something changed in his father's eyes, then was gone.

"You barged into an important meeting to talk about some woman you once knew?" Hugh asked angrily. "That's not good enough, Clayton. To interrupt an important business meeting for such a trivial reason is reprehensible."

Clay clasped his hands on the arms of the chair. If he lost his temper, he would lose a lot more. "Nicole isn't a trivial matter to me. She never was."

"Could you tell me," Hugh asked, using the reasonable, patronizing tone Clay hated, "why you feel compelled to bring up the subject of this woman at this precise moment? This couldn't wait until later? You amaze me, Clayton. You really do. The woman has been dead for over a year."

"I want to know how she died."

Hugh's eyes narrowed as he studied Clay carefully. "What possible difference could it make after all this time?"

"Humor me. Tell me how Nicole died."

"You know very well how she died, Clayton. Your car was hit on the passenger side and Miss Piccolo died of injuries sustained in the accident. Now, if you don't mind, I would like to get back to the board meeting. You've wasted enough of my time."

"Where is she buried?"

"I beg your pardon?"

"You heard me. Where is Nicole buried?"

Hugh stared at his son in silence for a moment. "I have no idea." The intercom on his left buzzed and he reached out to depress the button, welcoming the interruption.

Moving quickly, Clay sprang to his feet and

grabbed his father's hand. "No, damn you! No more delays. No more stalling. You're going to talk to me now."

"Clayton!" his father exclaimed, unable to disguise the fine thread of fear in his tone. "Have you lost your mind? You don't talk to me like this. I'm your father."

Clay leaned over the desk, his eyes as threatening as his stance, and replied, "You're the man who made a merger with my mother and bred a child. I have your blood in my veins and your name, but there's more to being a father than that." Straightening, he let his hands fall to his sides. "But I'm not here to discuss our family relationship, such as it is. I'm here to talk about Nicole. You lied to me about her and I want to know why."

"I've had quite enough of this inquisition. I have a business to run, and I don't have time to discuss some insignificant woman." Bracing his hands on the top of his desk, Hugh started to stand up.

"Sit down!" Clay ordered. "You aren't leaving this office until you explain why you told me Nicole was dead."

Hugh sat back down. With as much dignity as he could muster, he said, "I felt it was for your own good. You were spending too much time with her instead of with Ann Kimberly."

Clay gaped in astonishment. "What the hell difference does that make?"

"An association with Ann Kimberly would have been more beneficial," Hugh explained calmly. "Brian Kimberly of the Kimberly Corporation made it clear he would approve of his daughter's involvement with my son. You were dating her steadily until the Piccolo woman came along. By dropping Ann, you were jeopardizing the negotiations for a merger with the Kimberly Corporation. Brian Kimberly took it personally when you rejected his only daughter."

Clay shook his head in disbelief as his hands clenched into fists. "You told me Nicole was dead because of a business transaction?"

"Not entirely. You will evidently find this hard to believe, but I was thinking of your future as well. Marriage to Ann Kimberly would have provided you with the right connections and a great deal of money. Nicole Piccolo is the daughter of an actor. Her background would not have been beneficial to you socially or professionally."

Clay stared at his father. Even for him this was preposterous. He had calmly wiped out a woman because she was interfering with business. Lord, Clay thought wildly. What kind of man was he?

"Just for the record," he said, his voice as hard as steel, "Nicole Piccolo has more class in her little finger than Ann Kimberly has in her whole body. Nicole speaks several languages, has lived all over the world, and has attended a finishing school in Switzerland. Her father is not some two-bit actor in a sleazy sideshow. Abe Piccolo has been nominated for both an Oscar and an Emmy. But whether Nicole has the right credentials or not is none of your business. Nicole is *my* business, my personal business."

His father's expression remained passive, his opinion obviously unchanged.

Taking several deep breaths to try to gain control of his rage, Clay closed his eyes for a moment. A vision of Nicole with her smoky gray eyes and shimmering hair floated through his mind. His father had no idea what he had done. To Hugh McMasters, eliminating Nicole had been an expedient way of manipulating circumstances to fit his plans. Nicole had simply been a pawn that was sacrificed in order to win a more valuable piece in a commercial chess game.

Behind him, someone was knocking on the door and he heard the muted voice of his father's secretary as she called out Hugh's name. Getting no response, she banged harder on the door and rattled the doorknob, repeatedly calling out to her boss.

"Mrs. Abbott will call Security if I don't answer or open the door," Hugh said quietly.

Clay acknowledged the warning by nodding his head. "Just one more thing. What happened at the hospital? Did you say anything to Nicole?"

"No."

"Was she hurt in the accident?"

"I have no idea."

The pounding at the door equaled the pounding in Clay's temples. Through clenched teeth he asked, "You didn't even inquire about the other person in the car? I had a broken wrist, broken ribs, and cuts from glass, and you didn't think to check on the condition of my passenger?"

"She was no concern of mine."

Clay looked at his father steadily for a long moment. He had to get out of there. He had always known his father was an unfeeling bastard, but this topped even the most blatant manifestation of his callousness yet.

Clay went over to the door and unlocked it. After one last look at his father, he opened the door and pushed his way through the people gathered there. He wished someone had tried to stop him from leaving, as he was itching for a fight.

Nicole was alive, he thought as he stabbed the Down button for the elevator. He was going to find her if he had to take San Francisco apart brick by brick.

Several blocks away, Nicole leafed restlessly through a well-read magazine as she waited for the nurse to call her name. Her appointment had been for an hour ago, but she was still waiting. A doctor's office was not her favorite place, especially this doctor's office. To appease her concerned parents, though, she had kept her appointment for her six-month checkup.

Tossing the magazine onto a table, she shifted in her chair, attempting to find a more comfortable position but without much success. It was one of life's odd quirks that the waiting room of an orthopedic specialist would have chairs made from plastic Tinker Toys, she mused. With the kind of fees he charged, he could afford plush cushioned couches and chairs for the patients, especially since he made them wait so darn long.

On the other hand, she thought wryly, if all patients paid him as slowly as she did, he wouldn't be able to buy orange crates.

Staring at the clock on the wall opposite her,

she watched the minute hand tick slowly to the next second, then the next. If she wasn't called in soon, she was going to leave. She would give the doctor ten more minutes, then she would take off. She had better things to do with her time than waste it here. Like getting out of San Francisco.

She shifted her thoughts to the meeting she had had earlier with the director of the Unicorn Gallery. The shock of hearing him ask for more of her paintings, a lot more, had worn off, but not the glow of satisfaction. Painting had been a hobby for years and something to do while she recovered from her injuries after the car accident, and later from the corrective surgery on her leg. She had never considered her paintings could become a way to earn a living. Bless Aunt Jessie and her sneaky plots, she thought.

The director of the gallery had called her work "a flat-perspective primitive style." He could call it anything he wanted, she mused, so long as he was willing to sell her paintings. He had even mentioned the possibility of making prints and greeting cards in the future, depending on the success of her exhibit in November. If she could sell her paintings, it was a chance to be financially independent again.

Even if the doctor gave her a clean bill of health today, the chances of working in advertising again would be impossible, thanks to Clay McMasters. She could still remember the exact wording of the letter she'd received in the hospital from her employer, informing her that her services in the art department were no longer required. A phone call to a friend in the personnel department had provided her with the reason for her abrupt dismissal. One of the investors in the firm had requested she be fired. The investor's name? McMasters.

Even after all this time it was still a mystery to her why Clay would be so vindictive. Well, Clay McMasters could flat go to hell, she told herself. She was getting along just fine. More than fine. She was able to walk now, could drive a car again, and it finally looked as if she could earn a living. She certainly didn't need a man who could go away for a romantic weekend with her, make glorious love with her, and then disappear out of her life. Who needed that? Not her.

She picked up the magazine again. She wasn't going to think about Clay. She turned the pages of the magazine with more force than necessary. Thinking about Clay McMasters was a waste of time. For months after the accident she had gone over every word they had exchanged to try to find some reason why he had suddenly dropped out of her life, but she had come up with nothing that made any sense.

She turned the pages faster. No matter how she tried to stop them, the same questions kept repeating themselves. Would Clay have dropped her if they had been involved in the accident *before* they had made love? She closed her eyes as the most tormenting question persisted. Had she been that disappointing as a woman?

The sound of her name being called brought her back from her dark thoughts. The nurse was holding a thick medical file in her hand as she waited for Nicole to follow her to one of the consulting rooms.

An hour later Nicole left the office after being probed, poked, grilled, and stretched. The verdict was that her leg was as good as it was going to be. She had been told to exercise regularly, take the pain pills when she needed them, and to come back in six months.

As she waited for the elevator, she tore up the prescription for painkillers and threw it in a trash bin. The pain in her leg would be dealt with the same way she dealt with Clay's rejection, by gritting her teeth and getting on with her life.

While Nicole was driving over the Golden Gate Bridge to Sausalito to visit her parents, Clay was knocking on the door of the manager of the apartment building Nicole had lived in a year and a half ago. The manager couldn't give him any information regarding Miss Piccolo. Her parents had arranged for her things to be packed and taken away. He had no forwarding address for her.

Several hours later Clay wasn't any closer to finding Nicole. He had checked the hospital, the phone company, the electric company, and Nicole's former employer, but had come up with nothing, not a single lead. There was no listing for Nicole Piccolo with either the phone or electric company. The hospital refused to give any information about Nicole except to confirm she had been a patient there starting on the date of the car accident. They did tell him the name of her doctor, though.

Finally he went to his apartment to figure out what to do next. He unwrapped Nicole's paintings and stared at them as he went over everything he could remember about her, dredging up every fact, however trivial, eventually compiling several names. There were her parents, and aunt Jessie, and a close friend, Diana Dragas.

Even though he had never met any of these people, Nicole had talked about them. He had picked her up once at her parents' houseboat in Sausalito, but he wasn't sure he could remember which one of the over three hundred houseboats it was. Her parents hadn't been home then, but he knew her father was Abe Piccolo, a retired film star. That didn't help much. Abe Piccolo had an unlisted telephone number.

Her mother's sister, Jessie something-or-other, lived somewhere south of the city, around Santa Cruz, but he didn't know her last name.

Nicole's friend, Diana Dragas, lived in a houseboat next to the Piccolos'. Nicole had been friends with Diana for years. He remembered her telling him stories about their schooldays somewhere in Switzerland. Nicole had also told him about Diana's unusual job, but he couldn't remember where she worked.

Dammit! he thought. The only lead he had was her doctor. He doubted the doctor would tell him anything, but he had to try. He pulled out the thick San Francisco phone book and began searching the yellow pages.

The following day Nicole parked her car in front of her aunt's general store in a small community near Boulder Creek in the Santa Cruz Mountains.

She was tired from the three-hour drive from Sausalito, but she needed to report in to Aunt Jessie before she went home.

Jessie was a few years younger than her sister, Nicole's mother, but there was more than a few years of difference in the way they lived. Jessie had never married, and Rena had long been married to Nicole's father. Rena wore the latest fashions, and loved parties and traveling. Jessie preferred a quiet life in the mountains, content with wearing last year's slacks and sweaters, and considered three people a crowd. The sisters did have two things in common, though. Both were terrible cooks and both loved Nicole.

The bell clanged as Nicole opened the door, causing the clerk, Mrs. Piedmont, to glance up from the sack she was filling for a customer.

"Hi, Nicole. How was your trip to the big city?"

"Fine, Mrs. Piedmont."

"Your aunt's in the back."

Nodding, Nicole headed toward the doorway leading to her aunt's office and the storeroom. She stepped carefully around the displays in the aisles, concentrating on not favoring her leg. Mrs. Piedmont was a well-meaning snitch who would tell Jessie if she noticed Nicole limping.

A variety of familiar scents filled the air as Nicole strolled through the store. Jessie had kept the place basically as it had been for the last fifty years, complete with a pickle barrel, glass containers of candy, and yard goods pigeonholed on shelves in the wall. The counters, display cases, even the cash register were all from another time, another era, before stainless steel and chrome.

Ceiling fans stirred the air as they rotated lazily, one of them squeaking repeatedly.

Jessie was seated at her desk, a frown marring her usual serene expression as she tapped out a series of numbers on a calculator. Nicole knocked on the open door.

"Do you have a cup of coffee for a weary traveler?"

Looking up, Jessie smiled and waved her hand at the coffee urn in the corner of the small office. "Help yourself."

One of the many things Nicole liked about her aunt was she didn't fuss. She instinctively knew how much Nicole hated being pampered. Rena, on the other hand, still insisted on waiting on Nicole, even though she was perfectly capable of fending for herself now. During the visit with her parents yesterday, her mother had followed her around, stuffing pillows under her leg and continually asking her if she was all right. Nicole hated that question.

Pouring a cup of coffee, she asked, "Do you want a refill?"

Jessie shoved the calculator to one side and handed Nicole her cup. "You arrived just in time. I was about to throw this darn calculator into the pickle barrel. I'll never learn to do these blasted tax reports."

After she gave her aunt her cup back, Nicole sat down in the only other chair. "I'll do them tomorrow."

"If you have time," Jessie said, leaning back in her chair. "I was hoping you would come back with a large order for paintings from the gallery."

"Well . . ." Nicole drawled, grinning.

Jessie almost spilled her coffee as she lurched forward in her chair. "The gallery *did* ask for more paintings. Tell me everything. Every single word. Don't leave out a thing."

Nicole obliged, finishing with the possibility of having prints made of one of the paintings. "I think the director was a little disappointed when he saw me. He was probably expecting a Grandma Moses type. Now the only problem I can see is getting the paintings done by the November exhibition date."

"That's no problem. You simply paint like the dickens."

"Jessie, I have my work here, remember? I promised to help with your books, wait on customers, and stock the shelves in exchange for living in your cabin."

Jessie set her cup down and waved her hand in dismissal. "That was the arrangement before. Now you are to get out the old paintbrush and paint your little heart out."

"But Jessie . . ."

"I don't want to hear any of that rubbish about charity. I sent your paintings off for this very reason, to get you established as a recognized artist. You don't belong behind the counter the rest of your life."

"I can work here in the mornings and paint in the afternoon and at night."

"You can paint all day," Jessie said firmly. Then she smiled. "Of course, if you could manage to get my monthly tax statements done, I'll be forever in your debt."

"I'm already in yours, Jessie. More than I can ever repay," Nicole said sincerely.

Jessie felt about gratitude the same as Nicole felt about pity. "Nonsense. That cabin was empty. You're doing me a favor by living in it."

"That's not all and you know it." Nicole held up her hand to stave off the protests she saw building up in Jessie's face. "I know. You don't want to hear it, but when you save someone's life, you have to expect them to appreciate it."

"Posh," Jessie said, scoffing. "I didn't save your life."

"My sanity then. I would have lost it if I had had to stay in San Francisco when I got out of the hospital."

"I was selfish. I wanted the company." Glancing pointedly at her watch, Jessie asked, "Don't you have some brushes and paints waiting for you?"

Nicole smiled. "Yes, I do, as a matter of fact." She walked around the desk and kissed her aunt's cheek. "I'm going, but I'll be here in the morning to do the taxes." Taking something out of her large purse, she set it on the desk in front of Jessie. "I brought you some Ghirardelli's chocolate from San Francisco. If you make a batch of your famous brownies, I don't want to know about it." The one thing Jessie could make that was halfway decent was brownies. There was one time when she had gotten the salt and sugar mixed up, but usually the brownies were edible.

"There go my hips, but my taste buds thank you."

Nicole grinned. "See you later."

By the time she had unpacked her car, Nicole was too tired to bother fixing a hot meal. After she had a fire burning merrily in the fireplace, she opened a bottle of white wine to go with the cream cheese and freshly baked bagels she had purchased in San Francisco.

Propping her leg up on the couch, she looked at the stack of stretched canvases leaning against a box of other art supplies. For the first time in a long, long while she finally saw the light at the end of the tunnel. She would be able to make some money, perhaps enough to pay her parents back for what they had spent on her extensive hospital bills, and to pay off the doctor. Her parents didn't expect her to repay the money, but her pride made it necessary. Selling her paintings would go a long way to boosting her morale and self-esteem. Both had been dented badly after the accident had damaged her body and Clay's rejection had shattered her ego.

Bless Aunt Jessie, who always knew exactly what she needed. Two days after Nicole's last surgery Jessie had driven up to San Francisco and, ignoring Nicole's parents' protests, had put Nicole in her car and delivered her to the cabin in the mountains. Away from the smothering devotion of her parents, Nicole had been able to begin to heal her spirit as well as her body. Recently Jessie had sent the Unicorn Gallery one of Nicole's paintings in an attempt to get Nicole started on a new career. And as they say, Nicole thought, smiling, the rest is history.

Lifting her glass, she saluted the future, which for the first time in over a year was something to look forward to.

The following day Nicole took care of Jessie's tax statements, then stocked up on food supplies before settling down at her easel to paint. Several times, when she needed a break from her work, she went for walks in the woods to exercise her leg and to get some fresh air. Work, what a lovely word, she thought. It was wonderful to feel useful again.

She was up early the next day, her mind full of the painting she was working on, her fingers eager to pick up a brush. After completing the stretching exercises that had become a regular routine every morning and night, she showered, then dressed in jeans and slipped a faded red sweatshirt over a white shirt.

She was brushing her shoulder-length hair, when there was a loud knock at her door. A quick glance at the watch on her wrist showed it was barely eight o'clock. Jessie usually opened the store promptly at eight. Unless something was wrong.

Nicole hurried to the door, wondering why Jessie didn't walk in as she usually did. As she pulled open the door, the greeting intended for her aunt died on her lips when she saw who was standing on her doorstep. Every ounce of color drained from her face and she held on to the door as though it were a lifeline that could save her from falling into the familiar pair of dark eyes locked with hers.

Two

Clay hungrily drank in the sight of Nicole. He knew he was staring at her, but he couldn't stop. She looked even more frail than he remembered, a wraithlike figure as delicate as a wisp of smoke. She seemed the same, yet different. Her lovely eyes looked squarely at him, their color just as he remembered, except the laughter, the teasing light of mischief, were gone, replaced by shadows and something else he couldn't put a name to.

His gaze fell to her small hand clutching the door, and his body tightened as he remembered how she had made him feel when her hands had flowed over him as they made love.

With a strange huskiness in his voice he said, "Hello, Nicole."

Her smile was tight. "Hello, Clay."

He hadn't expected her to fall immediately into his arms, but he wasn't prepared for her cardboard greeting either. Her reaction told him several things, however. She was startled to see him, but not shocked, so she knew he hadn't been killed in the crash. It was also quite obvious she wasn't at all pleased to see him.

Her glance slid past his shoulder to the sports car parked in front of her cabin. "I see you replaced the car that was wrecked."

"The other car was totaled in the accident."

"You've bought another Porsche."

"I'm not here to talk about my taste in automobiles," he said, unable to hide his impatience entirely. "Are you going to invite me in?"

"No."

"Why not?"

'I'm busy."

His hands clenched in frustration. This wasn't going at all the way he had hoped it would. "I need to talk to you, Nicole."

Her surprise at finding Clay McMasters on her doorstep was beginning to wear off, and Nicole was finding her balance again. Placing her hand on her hip, she leaned against the doorframe.

"I can't think of a single thing I'd want to hear you say except good-bye." Her voice was casually sarcastic.

A muscle in Clay's jaw clenched. "I've been looking for you night and day for three days, Nicole. I'm not leaving now that I've found you."

Nicole didn't budge out of the doorway. She studied him carefully, noticing he did look tired. There were lines of exhaustion around his eyes and his mouth. His dark hair was mussed as though he had combed his long fingers through it numerous times. Underneath a gray leather jacket

he wore a white shirt with narrow blue stripes.
The shirt was rumpled.

Nicole found his rumpled shirt oddly fascinating. He had always appeared immaculately dressed
when he was with her before. She couldn't remember ever seeing Clay rumpled.

Crossing her arms under her breasts, she said,
"It's been over a year since the accident. I've been
here eight months, Clay, and you haven't found
any great need to talk to me before. How did you
find me, by the way?"

"I got the name of your doctor from the hospital. He wouldn't tell me anything, but"—Clay
smiled—"his nurse was very helpful."

That figures, Nicole thought. Clay could be dis-
armingly charming when he wanted. "What drove
you to track me down now?" she asked.

He played his ace. "I thought you were dead. I
learned only three days ago that you hadn't died in
the car accident. I've been looking for you ever
since."

His announcement didn't have the impact he
had expected. He saw her eyes widen in surprise,
then the distrust and wariness returned. Dammit! She didn't believe him.

"You thought I was dead," she repeated in mock-
ing tones. "Now, why would you think I was dead?"

"It's what I was told." He held back the part his
father had played after the accident. Since *he*
found it hard to believe, he certainly couldn't expect Nicole to believe it.

"Really?" she asked cynically. "Who told you
that?"

"It doesn't matter who told me. It's what I
believed."

"How did I die?" she asked curiously.

Parroting the phrase his father had used, Clay said, "From injuries sustained in the accident."

"I see. Well, your sources weren't as good as mine. The nurses at the hospital told me you had two broken ribs and a broken wrist. You also had two cuts on your face, but they weren't deep enough to leave scars. Several of the younger nurses were quite concerned about that." She scanned his attractive face. "It appears they didn't have anything to worry about. I was also told you had a concussion from hitting the side window, and that's apparently why you don't remember the lovely ride in the ambulance when I was on the stretcher next to you."

Her voice had a slight bite to it as she continued. "The nurses also let me know that you had been treated and released at your own request the day after the accident."

Without coming to see her, she added silently, as she lay in bed with two useless legs, one crushed and the other one broken, looking hopefully at the door every time it opened and pestering the nurses for any news about him. When she had been told he had left the hospital, hope had begun to wither. It died completely as days, then weeks passed without a word from him. When a lawyer brought a paper for her to sign to relinquish any claims against Clay McMasters because of the accident, she had known it was over between them.

"Well," she said, keeping her voice neutral, "as you can see, I'm very much alive and breathing. I'm also busy. What do you want?"

"I want you."

"For what?" she asked calmly.

Clay wanted to shake her. "For everything. I want to take up where we were before the accident. We're good together, Nicole. I want you back."

Nicole didn't know whether to slap his face or laugh herself silly at the nerve of the man. He honestly thought he could magically appear over a year later and announce that he wanted to continue where they had left off. *And* he expected her to believe his farfetched story about being told she had died. She may have given him the idea she was naive when he knew her before, but she was no longer the gullible woman who believed every syllable he uttered.

"You've been managing just fine without me since last summer," she said.

"Dammit, Nicole. I thought you were dead," he said heatedly. "I went through hell when I thought I'd never see you again."

She caught a momentary glimpse of pain in his eyes. She hoped to see it again, wanting him to hurt as much as he had hurt her. He had briefly looked like he *had* been through hell. Hell. She knew it intimately. She'd been there herself and she didn't want to make a return trip. He was the man who could send her there again—if she were dumb enough to let him do it.

"I'm sorry you've come so far, Clay, but I'm not interested in resurrecting something from the past. A lot of time has gone by, a lot of changes have been made. *I've* changed."

His mouth tightened. "Is there someone else?"

"I don't think you have the right to ask me

that." A fine thread of anger was weaving its way through her calm exterior. "You ignore me for over a year and now expect me to welcome you back with open arms. You get me fired from my job, send that pious lawyer to my room to sign a paper releasing you from any responsibility for the accident, and then you waltz up to my door expecting me to swallow some cock-and-bull story about thinking I had died. Why would you have a dead woman sign papers and fire her from her job? I haven't given much evidence of it in the past, but I'm not entirely stupid, Clay."

"What are you talking about?" he asked, completely mystified. "I never got you fired or had you sign any paper. I thought you had died in the accident."

Her angry outburst had taken a lot out of her, and she simply wanted him to leave. Seeing him again was bringing back too many memories she had tried hard to bury. "If you say so. I haven't the time or the inclination to stand here and argue with you. If you expect me to believe this story about thinking I was dead, I must tell you I've given up believing in Santa Claus and the Easter Bunny as well. I've outgrown fairy tales. It's over between us. Whatever we had I've put down to one of life's little jests."

Clay's eyes narrowed as he watched her. What was the signed release she babbled on about? And why did she think he had gotten her fired? Damn. Things were getting more complicated than clearer. He had the sinking feeling his father's fine manipulative hand was behind this.

She was so distant, so cold. Where was the

warm, sensual woman he had known? In an attempt to make some kind of contact with her, he lifted his hand to touch her cheek.

Her eyes wide with alarm, she flinched away from him, holding up her hand as though to ward him off.

He stared at her, shocked by her reaction. She wasn't as cool as he originally thought, he realized. He moved quickly toward her, clasping her arms as she automatically backed away from him.

His hands were gentle, his voice rough. "Let's see how much you've changed."

He held her firmly as he slowly lowered his head to cover her mouth with his own. Her gasp of panic and surprise was lost in the heat of his kiss, her struggles ignored as his arms went around her to bring her against him.

Molten heat jolted through Nicole as her body pressed into Clay's. There was a desperate hunger in his kiss, and he fed it by breaking open her mouth under his. When his tongue found hers, she panicked as a familiar ache began to grow deep inside her. Her hands went to his shoulders to push him away, but instead, her nails dug into his shirt and the flesh underneath as a torrent of emotions raced through her.

"I've missed you, Nikki," he murmured against her throat. "I've missed this."

She groaned against his warm mouth. She had missed this magic too. But magic was an illusion, easily conjured up and likely to vanish just as easily.

With a strength born from desperation, she shoved him away. With one last glance at him, she stepped back into her cabin and slammed the door.

Clay stood staring at her door. His first impulse was to knock it down and insist on talking to her. Now. This minute. In fact, he had gone so far as to raise his hand, but then he lowered it. Brute force wasn't going to endear him to her or make her listen to him. No matter how much she insisted it was over between them, she had responded to him. She hadn't wanted to but she had. Turning away, he walked back to his car. He needed time to convince her he was serious, time to untangle the misunderstandings between them. Somehow he had to find a way to get that time. Commuting was out. San Francisco was too far away. He had to think of some way to stay near her. He hadn't found her only to lose her again.

He sat behind the wheel of his car, his gaze on her closed cabin door. There was no way he could quit now. Whatever it took, however long it took, he would get her back.

He started the engine and drove down the dusty gravel road. Suddenly he shoved his foot on the brake, then reversed the car for a short distance. On his right was a faded sign on a post advertising a local real estate office. Tapping the steering wheel several times, he memorized the phone number painted under the name of the realty company.

A corner of his mouth curved up as he put the car in gear and continued along the road.

The deep throaty sound of Clay's car engine faded

away, and Nicole slumped against the door, letting out the breath she had been holding. As she walked into her studio she reviewed the last ten minutes. She was rather pleased with the way she had handled the unexpected meeting with Clay. He hadn't broken through the barrier she had erected over the past year.

Except when he had kissed her.

She consoled herself by rationalizing that she had responded to him only because she had been living like a nun for over a year. Determined to blot out the remembrance of how good it had felt to be in his arms again, she picked up a tube of paint and squeezed out a dollop of yellow ochre.

Suddenly she stared down at her hand, alarmed to find she was making a mess on her palette. Her hand was shaking! She dropped the tube of paint as though it had burned her fingers, then shoved her hand into her pocket and bit her lip in consternation. The barrier wasn't as impenetrable as she'd thought.

Well, she would start repairing the small crack in the wall. She wasn't going to be vulnerable to any man ever again. The highs weren't worth the lows. Being a gullible fool once was excusable. Twice was pure stupidity. Using the mortar of memory and the reinforcement of humiliation, Nicole painstakingly rebuilt her defenses.

She hadn't a clue why Clay had decided to come looking for her after all this time. It didn't make any sense. It also didn't matter. He was out of her life. Originally it had been his choice; this time it was hers.

She picked up another tube of paint, determined to get on with her painting without any further delay.

An hour later Nicole parked her car half a block away from her aunt's store. It was the closest space she could find. Grabbing her grocery list and purse, she opened her door. She had given up trying to paint. That little bird called doubt had perched on her shoulder, disrupting her concentration. Seeing Clay again had made her wonder if perhaps, just perhaps, she shouldn't have sent him away without listening to his explanation. No matter how many times she berated herself for being an idiot, she hadn't been able to banish him from her mind.

If anyone could keep her head out of the clouds and her feet firmly planted on the ground, it was Aunt Jessie.

Across the street Clay was standing at the window of the realty office while the realtor made a phone call. He couldn't believe his luck. When he had explained he wanted to rent a cabin or a house in the area, he hadn't expected the realtor to come up with a cabin so close to Nicole's. The cabin wasn't for rent, but the purchase price was relatively low. He didn't care what the price was. To be within walking distance of Nicole's cabin was more than he had hoped for. The realtor had implied that the cabin was not in prime condition, but Clay didn't care about that either.

His attention was caught by a woman with light hair as she stopped across the street to talk to an elderly woman who had just come out of the bakery. Nicole smiled at something the older woman said, then continued on her way.

Clay's eyes widened as he watched her walk. Nicole was limping!

The realtor, Mrs. Dickerson, put down the phone and came over to her new client. "Well, that's all taken care of, Mr. McMasters. You can move in as soon as the papers are signed. Today, if you'd like."

Receiving no reply, Mrs. Dickerson followed the direction of Clay's rapt gaze.

"As you can see, Mr. McMasters, our little community offers some lovely scenery," she said dryly. "That's Nicole Piccolo, who will be your new neighbor once you move into the cabin on the Low Road. She lives just above you on the High Road."

Clay's gaze followed Nicole's slender figure until she disappeared through the entrance of a building. The sign above the door read GENERAL STORE. Turning to Mrs. Dickerson, he asked, "What do you know about her?"

Mrs. Dickerson's eyes lighted up at the prospect of gossiping. She patted her hair, dyed a bright carrot-red, and plunged in. "Miss Piccolo moved here about seven, eight months ago." She gestured toward the store across the street. "That's her aunt's store. Jessica Carr has lived here for about twenty-five years. In fact, she owns a lot of property around here.

"No one saw much of Miss Piccolo at first. She was recovering from surgery to her leg. Something to do with a car accident she had been in." She paused when Clay gasped, then continued. "Apparently she had difficulty walking and her aunt had to take food to her until she was finally able to fend for herself. Now she helps her aunt in the store."

Mrs. Dickerson paused again and stared at him. "Are you all right, Mr. McMasters?"

No, Clay thought, he wasn't all right, but he wasn't about to admit it to this woman with the gleam of curiosity in her eyes. "Go on."

"About Miss Piccolo? Well, I heard her father is some movie actor, or maybe it was television. We don't see movies here unless we go to Boulder Creek, and television reception isn't too good unless you have one of those satelitte dishes, so I can't say I've ever seen this Abe Piccolo fellow. A few people around here have seen some of his movies, though. We all expected her to be kind of uppity. You know, daughter of a big movie star, but she's not." Her gaze remained intent on Clay's face. "She stays pretty much to herself. A couple of the local men have tried to interest her in going out with them, but she turns them all down."

Clay didn't want the realtor to know of his own interest in Nicole, so he simply said, "If you'll get the papers ready, I'll sign them. I want to leave for San Francisco this afternoon. I have a lot of arrangements to make."

"Of course. It won't take long to get them typed up. Would you like a cup of coffee while you're waiting?"

"No, thanks." What he wanted to do was march across the street and demand to know what in hell was wrong with Nicole's leg.

He gazed again at the store across the street, straining his eyes to see through the panes of glass to catch a glimpse of Nicole. Since the windows were crammed full of everything from baskets to blankets, with the occasional advertisement poster tacked here and there, it was impossible to see anything or anyone inside. Above the doorway was a date carved in wood. ESTABLISHED 1930.

Why would Nicole settle for working in a small country store when she'd had such a promising career in advertising? he wondered. Then he recalled her remark about having been fired, placing the blame for it on him.

How could he have gotten her fired when he had thought she was dead?

The questions kept coming without any answers. But that was going to change. It looked as if he needed to have another little chat with his father.

When Nicole entered the back room of the store, her aunt was sitting on the floor sorting through several boxes. Jessie glanced up, then moved one of the boxes out of the way to make room for Nicole to sit down. Once Nicole was seated, Jessie placed a box on her lap and said, "Sort these by holidays. Somehow the Halloween cards are mixed in with the Valentine's Day cards and the Christmas cards are everywhere."

Nicole began to sort through the box. For a few minutes the two women made various piles of cards on the floor without speaking.

When Jessie had emptied one box, she pulled another one toward her. "So what's up?"

"I had a visitor this morning."

"Why do I have the feeling it wasn't the Avon lady?"

Nicole smiled faintly. "It was Clay McMasters."

Jessie frowned. "McMasters. Where have I heard that name before?"

"Clay was driving the car I was in when the crash happened last year. I haven't seen him since the accident . . . until this morning."

Jessie tilted her head to one side. "Was that his decision or yours?" she asked quietly.

"His. It may not have been the kindest way to dump a lady after spending the weekend with her, but it was effective. I got the message loud and clear." Her mouth twisted in a rueful grimace. "It took a while for the message to filter through, but I finally got it."

Jessie took the box from Nicole and set it aside, her attention completely on her niece. "And?"

"And he came to my cabin this morning."

Nicole knew her aunt wouldn't let her get away with that oblique reply. Instead of insisting on any details, though, Jessie leaned back against some boxes and waited with her arms folded across her chest.

Nicole pulled her legs up and wrapped her arms around her knees. "This morning Clay told me he thought I had been killed in the car crash. Supposedly he discovered three days ago I hadn't died, so he found out where I was and trotted right up here to see me."

"You don't sound as though you believe him."

"Come on, Jessie. Would you? It's a little far-fetched. All I had to do in the hospital was ask one of the nurses about Clay's condition and I was told. He could have done the same thing. All he had to do was ask and he would have been told

I was alive. A little battered around the edges, but alive. I can't believe someone told him I had died. What would be the point?"

"None that I can see. There's an off chance a jealous girlfriend could have decided to eliminate the competition by killing you off, so to speak. One of the aides or a doctor could have gotten you mixed up with someone else. Didn't you say the woman in the car that hit you had been killed in the crash? Isn't it possible he could have been given the wrong information?"

"I suppose so."

Jessie let Nicole's doubtful reply go by without any further agreement. "So what does he want now?"

Nicole's mouth twisted. "He said he wants to get back together."

"How do you feel about that?"

Nicole leaned her head back against the large box behind her. "I don't know, Jessie. Heaven help me, I don't know. I thought I had gotten over him, until I opened my door and saw him standing there. Over the past year I've told myself Clay was just another man, but that's like saying a mink is just another coat."

"Do you think he'll be back?"

Nicole wished she could say no and believe it, but she remembered the look in Clay's eyes and the hunger she had felt in his kiss. He wasn't the type of man who gave up easily.

Slowly she nodded her head. "He'll be back."

Three

As the days crawled by without any sign of Clay, Nicole decided she had been wrong. Clay wasn't coming back. She began to wonder if she had imagined the moment on her doorstep or the flash of desire in his eyes when he pulled her into his arms. As she worked at her easel during the day or lay in her bed at night staring at the ceiling, she kept telling herself she was glad he was leaving her alone. She had recovered from the bout of infatuation she had felt for him a year ago. She was immune to tall, dark men who could melt an igloo with a smile and turn her bones to putty with a touch. Of course she was.

A week after Clay's visit Nicole was standing on her porch, reminding herself once again that she had done the right thing by sending Clay away. Who needed a man who could make her heart stop and her blood race? Not her.

A cool wind caused her to wrap her jacket tighter

around her as she looked out over the tops of the rustling pine trees on the slanting hillside in front of her cabin. She loved the view from her porch. There were trees as far as the eye could see, with only the rooftops of a few cabins indicating other inhabitants on the hill. The only cabin fairly close to hers was empty, and the other cabins were far enough away to give her the feeling of having the hillside all to herself. That was exactly the way she wanted it.

As her gaze roamed over the familiar view, there was a jarring note. Next to the empty cabin below she could make out the white roof of a long van. Apparently the cabin was no longer going to be empty.

Shrugging, Nicole went back inside. Whether she had a new neighbor or not, she had work to do. At least her paintings were going well. If she could keep up the pace, she would fill the order from the gallery without any difficulty. The painting she was working on now depicted a quilting bee with eight Amish women, and required a great deal of detail work. It was tedious, but she was enjoying every moment. The only problem was that she would get so wrapped up in painting, she would forget to get up and move around. Once in a while the cramped muscles in her leg would protest, reminding her she needed to take a break.

During one of her periods of exercise she heard a thudding sound coming from the back of her cabin. Then she heard the noise again. She took her jacket off the peg by the front door and slipped it on. Outside, she walked around to the rear of the house and saw a battered old pickup parked near the small storage shed. The thudding sound came from the other side of the shed. Moving carefully over the uneven ground, dodging the coarse clumps of grass, Nicole went around the corner of the shed.

For a moment she stood and stared. "Mr. Bascombe, what are you doing?"

The man chopping wood looked up. With his salt and pepper hair covered by a black knit cap, he could have been any age from forty to seventy. "I'm chopping wood."

"I can see that. Why are you chopping *my* wood?"

"I was told to." He swung the ax again, splitting a log.

Nicole was familiar with Mr. Bascombe's ways. He had done a few repairs around the cabin when she first moved in. He was a superior handyman but not much of a conversationalist. She came a little closer. "Who told you to chop my wood? My aunt?"

The ax fell again, neatly splitting a log in two. "No, ma'am."

Getting words out of Mr. Bascombe was like trying to pry a limpet off a rock, Nicole thought. "Then who did?" she asked patiently.

"Your new neighbor down the hill."

She stared at him. "My new neighbor! What are you talking about? I don't even know him . . . her. Why would they ask you to chop wood for me?"

Mr. Bascombe brushed a hand over several day's

growth of beard on his jaw and drawled, "Well, miss. You best take that up with that young man down the hill. I got work to do."

The ax was raised once again, the conversation over as far as Mr. Bascombe was concerned. Nicole retraced her steps back to the porch and looked down the hill toward the cabin below her. The moving van was no longer there. Mr. Bascombe must have gotten his instructions wrong, she told herself. Why would a stranger order firewood cut for her?

A sudden chilling thought struck her. Unless her new neighbor wasn't a stranger.

Slowly she began to walk toward the woods, wanting to know if her suspicions were correct and hoping they weren't. There had once been a path leading from her cabin to the one below, but it was overgrown with grass and littered with fallen limbs and rotting leaves. She carefully picked her way down the hill, finally reaching a clearing behind the cabin below hers.

There were no curtains in the windows and she couldn't see any signs of life through the dirty panes of glass. The log cabin and the area around it looked as unkempt and abandoned as it had always been. Then she walked around to the front and saw a familiar black Porsche parked in the gravel driveway.

Her heart thudded painfully in her chest. Her new neighbor was Clay McMasters!

The boards on the porch creaked under her weight as she approached the door. She knocked several times and was about to knock again when it opened.

Clay stood in the open doorway, a pair of jeans worn low on his hips, his feet and chest bare. He smiled at her, not at all surprised to see her.

Nicole's mouth went dry as her gaze flowed over his muscular chest, making it difficult to speak. "What do you think you're doing?"

Shrugging into a gray plaid shirt, Clay replied easily, "Getting dressed. I just took a shower. I had a battle with the wood-burning stove in the kitchen and it won. I was covered with soot."

Memories assaulted her of another time and another place, when she had joined him in a shower. She resolutely pushed them aside. "I mean, what are you doing here in this cabin?"

He gave her a faint smile as he buttoned his shirt. "Unpacking."

He moved away from the door, leaving it open. Nicole watched as he walked over to one of the boxes stacked in the living room and lifted a large metallic gray stereo component out of it. Then he dug back into the box, withdrew a bundle of wires, and proceeded to untangle them.

Dissatisfied with his answer, Nicole stepped over the threshold, fully aware that that was exactly what Clay wanted her to do. She looked around. An expensive tan and white sofa and matching club chair looked out of place against the dull log walls. An antique writing desk sat among bulging cardboard boxes in various sizes, its handsome pine finish already covered with a fine film of dust. The furniture looked new. The few lamps were still wrapped in plastic, and tags dangled from a table and one of the chairs.

Through a doorway she saw a double bed with the plastic wrapping still on the mattress and box spring. Clay had apparently purchased the bed specially for the cabin, since the king-size one in his apartment wouldn't fit into the small bedroom. Several suitcases stood on the floor and clothes on hangers were lying across the bed. A section of wallpaper was peeling off the wall and there was a water-stain darkening another area.

Her gaze came back to the main room. Some effort had been made to sweep the floor, but dust motes floated in the air and stubbornly settled over the boxes and furniture. Compared to Clay's apartment in San Francisco, this cabin wasn't even nice enough to call a dump.

"Clay, you can't be serious about moving here."

His attention remained on the wires in his hand. "I already have. Sit down if you can find a place. I'd offer you a cup of coffee, but I haven't found the coffeepot yet."

"I don't want any coffee. I want to talk to you."

This time he looked up, his expression unreadable. "You didn't want to talk to me last week when I came to see you. Why do you want to talk to me now?"

Biting her lip in frustration, she tried another tack. "You ordered Mr. Bascombe to cut firewood at my place. Why?"

He fit several plugs into the stereo unit before he replied. "You needed firewood. I heard your aunt talking about ordering Mr. Bascombe to get a supply of firewood in for you and I told her I'd take care of it."

"You *told* my aunt? How do you know my aunt?"

"I needed supplies. She looked at me as if I had three heads when I first introduced myself, but after a while she seemed to accept I was here for the duration. She's been fairly helpful. I met her when I stocked up on groceries." He briefly scanned the room. "I wish I could remember where I put them. I could use a cup of coffee."

He held up an electrical plug. "There's an outlet over there behind that box. Will you plug this in? I want to see if I did this right."

Muttering under her breath, Nicole did as he asked. Once the stereo was plugged in, Clay inserted a cassette tape and flicked a couple of switches. The room filled with the voices of the Pointer Sisters. Clay scooted over to delve into another box as the throbbing music echoed throughout the small room.

Nicole had to raise her voice to be heard. "Dammit, Clay! This is ridiculous. You can't live here."

He turned down the volume on the stereo. "This place may not look like much right now, but with a little work it will suit me just fine." He unwrapped some paper from a coffeepot and held it up in triumph. "Now, if I can find some cups and the coffee, we're in business."

"I don't want any blasted coffee. I want some answers. I want to know why you moved here. If it's because of me, you can start packing everything back in the boxes. I'm doing just fine, thank you. I don't need you here to order my firewood or complicate my life."

For a long minute Clay didn't respond. Then he

set the coffeepot down on the floor beside him. "It looks like you'll have to adjust, Nikki, because I'm not going anywhere. If we have to start over, then that's what we'll do. I've lost over a year with you. I'm not losing another minute."

Her eyes widened in astonishment. "You're mad."

A corner of his mouth slowly curved up into a smile. "Mad as in angry, not crazy. But not at you, Nicole. Never at you."

Plopping down onto the sofa, she said wearily, "I don't understand."

"I know you don't. Maybe in time you will." Thinking of his father's part in all this, he added, "Maybe someday I will too."

"So whether I want you to or not, you're going to stay here."

"For however long it takes."

"Until when?"

"Until you trust me again."

She met his intent gaze. "You are in for a long wait."

Something stirred in his eyes and then was gone. He moved over to another box and ran a knife along the taped seam. "Then I'd better make this place more comfortable, hadn't I?"

Nicole leaned back on the sofa, watching his every move, hoping to find some clue to explain his actions.

"What about your business, Clay? There isn't a great need for financial consultants here in the mountains."

"My partner is taking over. I've taken a leave of absence."

She gaped at him. He gave her a half smile and continued his unpacking. Dear Lord, she thought. He was serious. She was afraid to let herself believe he wanted her again after so much time had elapsed. It was going to be difficult enough to fight the attraction she knew was still there between them. She didn't want to have to fight herself as well.

It had been nearly impossible to banish him from her mind during the past year, and then he hadn't been living a stone's throw from her cabin. Whatever he wanted from her, she wasn't going to give it to him.

Clay continued to empty the box in front of him. Every cell in his body was aware of Nicole sitting only a few feet away. This idea of his better work, and soon. Somehow he had to keep his hands off her, but it wasn't going to be easy. He wondered what her reaction would be if he told her he hadn't been with a woman since the weekend they had shared together over a year ago. She wouldn't believe him. She would probably fall off the sofa laughing. Why would she believe that when she didn't believe anything else he said? But she would.

By the time he had emptied the box, he was surrounded by paper and the small oblong boxes he had unpacked. He stacked the small boxes carefully before stuffing all the papers back into the large box.

The way he took so much care with the boxes made Nicole curious. "What's in the boxes?" she asked.

Gathering them up, Clay got to his feet. As he passed her on his way toward the desk, he dropped one of the boxes in her lap. "See for yourself."

She lifted off the lid. "It's a harmonica," she said in astonishment.

"I know." There was amusement in his voice.

"Do all those boxes contain harmonicas?"

He set them on the desk, then turned around. "So far I have eighteen."

She looked at him as if she had never seen him before. In a way it was true, she thought. She had never seen this side of him before. "You have eighteen harmonicas? Why?"

"When I was eight, I went away to summer camp and one of the counselors had a harmonica. He would play it at night when we gathered around the bonfire. I was fascinated by the way he could make that small instrument cry or laugh, depending on what he played and how he played it. By the end of the summer I could play a couple of simple songs. Over the years I've learned a few more songs and somehow ended up with eighteen harmonicas."

She continued to stare at him. "I didn't know you could play a harmonica."

"There's a lot about me you don't know, Nicole," he said quietly. "When we were together before, we communicated on a physical level. I realized that we didn't really know each other very well when I tried to find you a week ago. I knew the names of your parents and your friend, Diana Dragas, but I had never met them. I went back over every conversation we ever had to find a clue to where you might be. I was shocked to realize we hadn't shared much of ourselves except in bed. I'm here to change that."

Nicole gazed down at the shiny metal harmonica she still held in her hand as she absorbed his words. Sometime during the past year she had come to the same realization that he had. "We can't change the past, Clay."

"True, but we can change the future." He saw the guarded look in her eyes when she raised them to meet his. "For over a year we've traveled alone over two separate roads. Right now we'll be living on two different roads. I want us to walk, talk, and live on the same road."

He let his words soak in. It was too soon to push her any further. He had planted a seed and it would take time for it to grow. He wanted to ask about her injuries from the accident. He wanted to demand to know why she still limped a year after the accident, but he knew she wouldn't tell him. She didn't think he had any rights where she was concerned, which was probably true. But he would earn the right to know everything about her.

He walked over to two large flat objects wrapped in brown paper leaning against one of the walls. "While you're here, you could give me advice on where these paintings would look best."

Nicole placed the harmonica back into the box and got up to set it with the others. She didn't want to get involved in decorating this poor excuse for a cabin. "I really should be going."

"This won't take long." In a few minutes he had the paper off the paintings and held one up for her to see. "I'd like to hang this one in the bedroom."

Nicole stared at the familiar painting, at Clay, then at the other painting facing the wall. "Is that other one mine too?"

"Yes."

Slowly she walked over to the second painting and turned it around. "You've been to the Unicorn Gallery."

"That's how I discovered you were alive. I recognized this painting in the window. I remembered you had it hanging in your apartment. When I went into the gallery to purchase it, I found out you had an exhibit coming up. Since I thought you were dead, it was quite a revelation."

She let the painting fall back against the wall. "Don't start that again," she snapped.

"Start what?"

"That bit about my being dead. It's lost its shock value."

"Not to me it hasn't." He edged closer to her and lifted his hand to touch her face. "I know you find it hard to accept that I thought you were dead, but it's true. The person who told me was also responsible for sending the lawyer to your room and arranged for you to lose your job. I did some checking when I got back to San Francisco after you hit me with those accusations."

"Who was it?"

A strange sadness clouded his expression briefly. "It doesn't matter. The important thing is I've found you again. I always thought everyone was entitled to one miracle in his life, and I've had two. The first one was when I met you over a year ago, and the second was that day in the gallery when I learned you were still alive."

Nicole was unable to look away from his intent gaze as his fingers remained under her chin, his thumb smoothing over her jaw. She had seen that expression before in his eyes, a look that said she was the most precious thing on earth. She had once reveled in that look. Now she didn't trust it.

Seeing the wariness in her eyes, Clay dropped his hand and stepped away from her. "So," he said, with a hint of hoarseness in his voice, "are you going to help me hang these paintings or not?"

Somewhere during the last few minutes Nicole had forgotten to breathe and her chest hurt as she drew air into her starved lungs. She felt as though she were being swept into a whirlpool of forgotten feelings and emotions.

Remembering the pain of his rejection, she said abruptly, "Not. I want you to take the paintings, your harmonicas, and everything else you've brought with you and go back to San Francisco. I don't want you here. I don't want you within fifty miles of me. I don't know what game you're playing and I don't want to know. I just want you away from here."

He lowered the painting to the floor. "I'm staying, Nicole. I'm going to live in your back pocket."

She threw up her hands in frustration. "Why? What we had is over, Clay. History."

"It's only beginning."

She wasn't getting through to him. Nothing she said was making any difference. She headed toward the door. "Then start without me."

He moved quickly to block her exit. "I've been without you for over a year, Nicole. Never again."

His hands closed on her arms and he pulled her against his body. His mouth closed over hers, his tongue forcing her lips apart. No other woman felt like Nicole, tasted as feminine or as desirable as Nicole. There was no other woman for him but Nicole. There never would be.

Nicole struggled with herself to fight the sensual pleasure she felt in his arms. His tongue surged into her mouth to mate with hers and her fingers clenched his shirt as she seemed to be drowning in sensation after sensation. Flaming passion ignited her nerve endings and she trembled.

His hands slid down her back to press her hips into his. A jolt of desire weakened her knees and her resolve when she felt his aroused, hard body against hers.

"Let me go, Clay," she pleaded as he rained brief, hot kisses over her throat. "I don't want this."

Clay heard the desperation in her voice. Reluctantly allowing her to draw a little away from him, he raised his head and cupped her face between his palms.

"I hear what you're saying, but your body is telling me something different."

Slowly his lips moved over hers in a blatantly sensual kiss. When he at last looked up again, he whispered, "You want me, Nikki. We belong to-gether. I've already convinced your body. Now I have to convince your pride."

Nicole forced herself to shove him away. Her gray eyes were sad and weary. "My pride was all I had left after the accident, Clay. I'm not going to let you take that too."

She walked around him and opened the door before he was able to stop her, then strode quickly into the woods to return to her cabin.

Clay didn't follow her.

Four

There was no sign of the usual early morning fog
blanketing the valley as Nicole sat on the front
steps of her cabin a little after seven the morning
after her visit to Clay's cabin. She cupped the
mug of hot coffee between her hands and looked
out over the peaceful valley.

The air was brisk but not uncomfortably cold.
She was warm in the waist-length jacket she wore
over a white Irish-knit sweater, the collar of the
jacket turned up around her neck.

The morning light she had waited for during
the long sleepless night had finally arrived. She
might not have gotten much sleep last night, but
she had gotten a lot of painting done. She preferred to make the night go by faster by keeping
busy rather than staring up at the ceiling above
her bed and accomplishing nothing.

Sipping her coffee, Nicole felt a sense of déjà vu.
There had been many mornings in the past just

like this one, when she had waited for the dawn on these same steps. This cabin had been her sanctuary, her retreat, where she could heal physically and emotionally in private. Gradually she had managed to sleep the whole night through without waking in a cold sweat, her leg on fire, her muscles screaming for relief. The tortured dreams of being in Clay's arms had also faded. She had really thought she was through with all that.

She leaned back against one of the heavy posts supporting the porch roof. This whole thing with Clay had to be faced, she thought. Losing sleep wasn't going to solve a thing. She had to figure out what to do about him. Was he telling the truth? she wondered. All of a sudden he had moved bag, baggage, and harmonicas to a nearby cabin after telling her he had thought she'd died in the car crash. As outlandish as his claim sounded, she found it difficult to believe he would make up a story like that. What would be the point?

She told herself that she might as well accept the fact that he wasn't going to go away just because she asked him to. There wasn't anything she could do about him staying in the cabin, but there was something she could do about her reaction to seeing him. Besides, she had discovered her curiosity was greater than her resentment. She needed to know if her judgment had been so wrong before. One of the hardest facts she had been forced to accept was that Clay must not have cared for her as much as she had come to believe.

During the weekend they had spent together, he had shown her a degree of companionship and lovemaking she had never known before. Nothing had been said about any plans for a future together, but Nicole had assumed they had a future. She had seen him as a man of high standards, integrity, and self-confidence. Could she have been so wrong about him?

Several birds suddenly took flight from the trees near the edge of the woods and she heard a twig snap. She wasn't at all surprised when a familiar tall figure emerged from the woods and headed toward her. She had known he would come eventually.

When he got close enough so she could see him clearly, she noticed Clay looked like she felt. Either his new mattress didn't suit him or he had spent the night unpacking instead of sleeping. The tails of the red wool shirt he wore over his white T-shirt weren't tucked into his tight jeans but hung out over his lean hips. His eyes were dull with fatigue, his hair mussed as though he had combed his fingers through it a number of times. In one hand he held an empty coffee mug.

"I still can't find the coffee I bought yesterday," he said. His voice was husky and bordered on grumpy.

Nicole couldn't help smiling at his petulant tone, although she covered it by turning her head toward the cabin door and gesturing with her hand. "Help yourself."

His boots clumped heavily on the wooden steps and then the porch. As he opened the cabin door he mumbled something which Nicole accepted as a thank-you.

Against her will her smile broadened. Seeing

Clay muddled and untidy was rather endearing. When she had known him in San Francisco, he had always been at his best. Best clothes, best manners, and best places were what she had come to expect. This Clay was more vul-nerable than the one she had thought she'd known, more human, more approachable. Or had she seen only what she wanted to see be-fore? Everything had happened so fast between them. From the moment she had met him, she had been caught up in an attraction too powerful to allow her to think, only to feel.

Her mouth twisted in self-mockery. Of course, there was nothing like a good old-fashioned case of lust to keep a girl from thinking about anything but the man whose mere touch turned her mind to jelly and her body to flames.

Suddenly she frowned. He was taking his sweet time getting a simple cup of coffee. Her cabin wasn't that large nor the coffeepot that hard to find. She started to get up to check on what was taking him so long, when the door opened and Clay came out.

The boards in the porch creaked in protest as he sat down beside her. He held his steaming coffee mug in one hand and was contentedly munching on a bagel. "When I said to help yourself," Nicole muttered, "I meant the coffee."

Clay studied her thoroughly, wondering if she was seriously objecting to his free use of her food or whether she was protesting just to be protesting. He decided on the latter. "It's a little late to be standing on ceremony, isn't it? I saw you every

day for three weeks and lived with you one weekend."

"We weren't living together!"

"We ate together, slept together, my clothes hung
next to yours in the closet, and we shared a bathroom. That sounds like living together to me."

It sounded like it to her too. She knew she was
overreacting to the slightest thing he said or did.
It wasn't doing anything except making her look
and feel incredibly foolish. "It doesn't matter."

"On the contrary. I think our living together
matters very much."

"I meant it doesn't matter that you helped yourself to the bagel," she said in exasperation. In an
attempt to find a safer topic than their past relationship, she asked, "Am I correct in assuming
you can't find any of your groceries, not just the
coffee?"

"You would be correct." He finished off the last
bite of the bagel, washed it down with coffee, and
decided he was going to live after all. "I looked
everywhere, even under the bed. I know I bought
groceries at your aunt's store. I just can't find
them."

"Did you look in your car?"

He jerked his head around, staring at her as if
she had just said something profound. "I didn't
think to look there. They're probably still in the
trunk."

"I hope you didn't buy anything that will spoil."

He smiled faintly. "I didn't see anything resem-
bling a frozen dinner at your aunt's general store.
I bought mostly canned goods."

"Frozen dinners are from this century. Aunt Jessie doesn't think much of them. She's rather old-fashioned."

"I noticed." Especially when it came to the men in her niece's life, he mused. He hadn't been grilled that thoroughly since he had been questioned by his high school principal about the broken window in his office. It hadn't been easy but he had finally convinced Nicole's aunt he had been telling the truth about thinking Nicole had died in the car crash. Her aunt now believed he really cared for Nicole and hadn't returned to hurt her again. Somehow he had to convince Nicole.

He leaned his arms on his bent knees and gazed out at the scenery. "I can see why you like it here, Nikki. It's very beautiful." He turned his head to look at her, his gaze steady and unwavering. "It suits you somehow."

A spark of mischief brightened her gray eyes. "I can't say the same about you. I don't think this country setting is quite your element."

"Why? Just because I misplaced a few bags of groceries? I don't stay in the city all the time. If you remember, I took you to a cabin in Marin County that was definitely out of the city."

Maybe it was because her senses were becoming increasingly dull with fatigue, but his reference to their weekend together didn't bother her as much this time. "We didn't exactly rough it that weekend, Clay," she said with some amusement. "The cabin had every modern convenience complete with our meals delivered to the door by the staff at the lodge. There are no housekeepers, doormen, or waiters here. This is real life. If you're hungry, you fix yourself something to eat. If you're cold, you build a fire. Everyday life is more basic here in the mountains."

He gave her a long, assessing look. "Are you telling me what we had before wasn't real? It felt damn real to me. I admit to fulfilling a few male fantasies when I made love to you, Nikki, but the lovemaking was definitely real between us."

Her eyes suddenly darkened with memories, and she couldn't look away from him.

His voice was soft and husky as he gave her a slow smile. "Honey, don't look at me like that or I'm not going to be able to continue being what you want me to be."

She was unable to control her breathing, and her voice wavered. "What do I want you to be?"

"An acquaintance. A friend, not a lover," he said with a lightness he was far from feeling. "You don't trust me enough to be my lover again, so we'll work on being friends."

"We don't have to be anything at all. You could go back to San Francisco."

Leaning over, he kissed her quickly. "Not unless you go back to San Francisco too. You're stuck with me, sweetheart. You might as well accept it." Then, changing the subject abruptly, he said, "When I went in to get my coffee, I looked at some of your paintings. I gather you've been busy."

Feeling slightly dazed, Nicole answered automatically, "I have an exhibit coming up in November. It requires a lot of paintings."

"You must be putting in some long hours." He glanced at her. "I saw your light on late last night."

Nicole remembered her aunt had once said that

if you aren't driving the car, you haven't much say as to where you're going, so you might as well enjoy the ride. From experience, Nicole knew it would always be a bumpy road with Clay, but she had missed trying to keep up with the detours his conversations could take. "You must have X-ray vision. You can't see my cabin from yours."

He swallowed the last of the coffee and set the mug down beside him. "I went for a walk around midnight to get some fresh air." His sharp gaze scanned her face, then with one finger he traced the shadows of fatigue under her eyes. "I hope this is from working late on your paintings and not because of me."

She moved her head away from his hand, not because she didn't like his touch, but because she liked it too much. Her reaction made her angry. "Don't flatter yourself, Clay. My lack of sleep doesn't have anything to do with you being here. I was painting during the night because of the up-coming exhibit."

In a way he was disappointed at her answer. He would like to have her a little bothered by his presence. Heaven help him, she was all *he* could think about. Knowing she was just up the hill from his cabin had kept him from sleeping, and instead he had paced outside her cabin in the middle of the night.

"This exhibit is important to you, isn't it, Nikki?"

"Of course it is. It's my first one." Unconsciously she began to rub her leg. "It can either be a success or a big bomb."

Clay saw her stroking her thigh. He pushed himself off the steps, then reached down for her hand and pulled her up beside him. "Come and walk with me. I need to stretch my legs."

"I don't want to go for a walk."

"Nikki," he said wearily. "You don't have to fight me on every little thing." He tugged on her hands. "Come on. Walk with me."

She scowled at him. "I really don't see how I've managed to get along all this time without you telling me what to do."

He smiled down at her. "It is amazing."

"You're too used to having your own way, Clay McMasters."

His smile slowly faded as he thought about his father and their strained relationship. "Not always."

They started toward the woods, and Nicole tried to walk without limping. She slanted a quick look at Clay, but he was gazing at the surrounding trees. He appeared deep in thought, and by his expression they weren't pleasant thoughts. He had automatically taken her hand, threading his fingers through hers, and she didn't attempt to pull away. She felt he needed comforting, which seemed odd, but the feeling persisted. Why would he need comforting?

For a few minutes they walked in silence. Then Clay said casually, "While I was in San Francisco making arrangements to move here, I talked to your boss at Steiner's."

She whipped her head around to stare at him. "My ex-boss," she said briskly. "I don't work there anymore."

"You can if you want to."

She stopped and turned to face him, pulling

her hand from his without any resistance from him. "You talked him into hiring me back? Why?"

"So you would have a choice. If this exhibit is what you really want to do, fine, but if it's what you're settling for because you were fired from the agency, that is no longer a problem."

"Why the change of heart?"

His mouth tightened into a thin line. "I'm not the one who got you fired, Nicole," he said, and his voice was hard and gritty. "I already told you that, but you didn't believe me. I don't have that kind of clout even if it was something I wanted to do."

"I was told a Mr. McMasters had insisted I be fired. You're the only McMasters I know. What else was I supposed to think?"

"I'm not the only McMasters in San Francisco."

Her eyes searched his, and she wondered why he sounded so bitter. "You mean someone in your family? Why would a member of your family want me to lose my job?"

He shook his head. "It doesn't matter who or why." He took her arm and began walking again, bringing her along with him. "I've straightened out the misunderstanding with Mr. Steiner. You can go back to work at the agency or he will give you a recommendation if you want to work for any other agency. It's up to you."

Nicole still didn't understand why anyone in Clay's family would go to the trouble of getting her fired from her job. She didn't know any McMasters but Clay. It didn't make sense. Right now it also didn't matter whether it made sense or not. Whatever Clay's motives were for talking to her ex-employer, it didn't change anything. She told him so.

"I don't want to go back to the agency. I want to see if I can make a living selling my paintings." She didn't tell him that physically she wasn't able to keep up with the fast pace an advertising agency would demand. She paused for a long moment, looking up at him, then said quietly, "I don't understand what's going on, but I appreciate your clearing things up with Mr. Steiner. I didn't like losing my job, especially when I didn't know why."

"I don't imagine you did."

"I still don't know why," she said, fishing for a reason.

He helped her around a large shrub and held back a low-hanging branch for her to pass under. He remained silent.

"You aren't going to tell me, are you?"

"You haven't believed anything I've said so far," he responded calmly. "I told you I thought you had died in the car accident and you still don't believe it. Why would you believe anything else I tell you?"

Nicole had been looking up at him and not at where she was going. Her toe caught on an exposed root and she would have fallen if Clay's hand hadn't automatically tightened on her arm and held her up. Off balance, she put too much weight too suddenly on her bad leg. A short gasp escaped from her before she bit her lip to keep from crying out.

A large fallen log was a short distance away, and Clay led her there, his arm supporting her.

"I'm all right," she said heatedly as he forced

her to sit down. She was angry for tripping, angry at her injured leg, angry with Clay for being there. She started to get up, but he restrained her by holding her arm as he sat down beside her. "I'm all right," she repeated.

"I can see that." He began to stroke the tense muscles of her arms. "You've never been better. It's only my imagination that you're biting your lip and your hands are clenched into fists."

Making a concentrated effort, Nicole relaxed her hands. She rested her palms on her thighs, resisting the temptation to rub her aching leg. In a calmer voice she said, "I'm fine, really."

Clay's hand stilled on her arm. "We'll sit here until you're better than fine."

He realized that both he and Nicole had boundaries that they weren't prepared to let the other cross. His boundary was the subject of his father, and Nicole's, he knew now, was her injured leg. She had lowered her wall of distrust slightly, but it was still between them enough to prevent revealing what was behind the barrier.

For a few minutes they sat on the log in silence. Nicole could sense Clay's curiosity, but she wasn't ready to tell him about her injury. During the long night she had wondered if Clay had returned to see her out of belated guilt over the car accident. If he knew how serious her injuries had been, it would only compound his guilt. She didn't want guilt from him, or pity. The problem was, she didn't know what she did want from him.

Clay wanted to pick Nicole up in his arms and carry her back to her cabin, but he instinctively knew her pride wouldn't allow it. He hoped to heaven he could come up with the patience to give her the time she needed to trust him again. He could demand to know how serious her injury had been, but he knew he didn't have that right. Yesterday in his cabin she had said her pride was all she had left after the accident and he wasn't about to take any of it away from her.

When he felt her arm relax under his hand, he asked, "Do you want to go back to your cabin or do you want to continue walking in the woods?"

Getting to her feet, she tentatively put some weight on her bad leg and was relieved the pain was only slight. "Back to the cabin. I need to get to work."

This time Clay didn't take her arm or attempt to touch her in any way, although he was aware of every step she took and was ready to reach out for her if she stumbled again. If it were up to him, he would knock down every obstacle in her path, literally and figuratively.

At the cabin steps she turned to face him. "Don't forget the groceries that are still in your car."

He was being dismissed and he knew it. "I won't. Thanks for the coffee."

"You're welcome."

For a few tense seconds their eyes were locked together. Finally Clay smiled faintly and said, "I'll see you later."

Nicole managed a slight nod and watched him as he strolled toward the woods, then was finally out of sight.

Nicole worked straight through the morning and afternoon, not stopping for lunch and eating only a sandwich at nine in the evening. She had taken

several breaks from her painting to walk around
the cabin when her leg insisted on some exercise,
but the rest of the time was devoted to her work
in an effort to keep her mind away from the riot of
emotions inside her.

A little after ten that night she cleaned her
brushes and got ready for bed. She was too tired
to paint anymore. She had begun to make too
many mistakes, mixing the wrong colors and dis-
torting some of the figures. After doing her exercises, she slipped on a long white satin nightgown
and slid between the cool sheets on her bed. Now
that there was nothing to occupy her mind, she
found herself thinking about the cabin below hers.
She wondered if Clay was warm enough, whether
he had managed to get the old stove to work so he
could prepare something to eat. She wondered
what he was doing, if he was thinking about her.
Irritated with her wayward thoughts, she punched
the pillow several times and ordered herself to
stop being a complete idiot and go to sleep.

She willed her body to relax. The dull ache in
her leg was constant and pervasive, though, wearing away her tolerance. Her long spell of painting
was catching up to her and she was going to have
to pay for accomplishing so much by having to
endure the pain in her leg.

By one o'clock in the morning she was still
awake. She had pulled a white robe on over her
nightgown and was pacing the floor of her living
room to try to work out the pain. It had gotten
progressively worse as the hours passed, making
it impossible for her to rest.

Unable to sleep himself, Clay walked up the path toward Nicole's cabin. When he saw the light in her window, he felt an unreasonable anger that she was still painting at this late hour instead of resting. As he neared the cabin, he saw her slight figure cross in front of the window and then return. Going up to the window, he looked in and saw the lines of strain around her mouth and the sheen of perspiration on her face as she limped around the room, her hand rubbing her thigh.

To hell with patience and waiting, he thought. He ran up the steps and tried the door, only to find it locked. He pounded on it. "Nicole, let me in!"

There was a brief silence, then she yelled at him through the closed door to go away. His fist struck the door again several times. "Nikki, either let me in or get out of the way, because I'm going to break down your door."

Exasperated, exhausted, and completely fed up with her leg, herself, and the damnable situation caused by Clay's return to her life, she limped painfully over to the door and yanked back the bolt. Opening the door enough to see him, she said angrily, "Go away, Clay. It's—"

He ignored her protests. As soon as the door was unlatched, he began to move. He swept her off her feet and carried her over to the couch. Setting her down gently, he carefully arranged her legs on the cushions. He nudged her hips over to give him room to sit on the edge of the couch, his arms braced on either side of her, forcing her to stay put.

In a quiet but firm voice he asked the question that had been burning in his mind ever since he had first seen her limping. "What's wrong with your leg?"

She wanted to say there was nothing wrong, but under the circumstances, she knew it was ridiculous to try to fool Clay. She was so tired of fighting the pain and fighting him, and she sighed heavily. "Both legs were broken in the accident. One worse than the other."

"And?"

Frowning, she asked impatiently, "And what?"

"The accident happened a long time ago. Why is your leg still bothering you?"

Resigned, Nicole related the details. "When my side of your car was hit, my legs were forced up against the gearshift. My left leg was broken in three places, my right leg only had one break. The broken bones have healed, but the left leg had to have several operations because some of the muscles in the thigh were damaged. Occasionally the muscles go into spasms or cramp up."

"Like now?"

She nodded. "I . . . ah, painted too long without taking a break today." She saw his mouth tighten and hurriedly added, "I'll be all right in a little while. You don't need to stay. I can take care of myself. I'm used to it."

His only response was a look of complete exasperation accompanied by a slight shaking of his head. Standing up, he said warningly, "Stay there."

Nicole stared after him as he walked into the small kitchen. She couldn't see what he was doing but she could hear water being poured into a tin container. Several of her cupboard doors were opened and shut, then she heard the clinking of glass against glass. He came back into the room carrying a small glass containing a dark liquid.

"Have you taken any medication for your leg?" he asked.

She shook her head.

"Do you have a heating pad?"

Again she shook her head.

He handed her the glass. "All I could find was this brandy. Drink it. It'll relax you."

After he had made sure she had taken a few sips of the brandy, Clay returned to the kitchen. Nicole took several more healthy swallows, coughing as the brandy burned all the way down. In a few minutes he came back holding a steaming basin, which he set on the floor. Hunkering down beside the couch, he swept back her robe and nightgown until her thigh was exposed, completely ignoring her indignant protests.

"Let me know if this is too hot," he said. "This will work best if you can stand it hot, but I don't want to burn you."

He lifted a folded towel from the basin and wrapped it around her left thigh. His gaze went to her face when he heard her gasp. "Is it too hot?"

"No. It startled me, that's all."

His hands moved to her thigh and he felt her tense under his fingers. "Just relax. I won't hurt you."

His fingers began to massage her thigh, first on top of the towel and then under it, rubbing gently at first, then with more strength in each soothing stroke. Nicole wanted to close her eyes and give in to the delicious ministration of his fingers, but she felt she should protest out of principle . . . or something.

"Clay, you don't need to do this because you feel guilty about the car accident."

His fingers stopped for a brief moment, then resumed the magical massage. "I don't feel guilty about the car accident. It wasn't my fault."

"I just thought . . ."

"I know what you thought. You've been thinking a lot of things that are completely wacky. Right now I'm *feeling* a lot of things, Nikki, especially under the circumstances." His hand stroked higher on her thigh, almost to her bare hip, then back down toward her knee. His voice had changed to a low sensual drawl. "Believe me, guilt isn't one of them."

Her leg wasn't the only thing being stroked, Nicole thought. The faint embers of passion that had never been completely extinguished during the last year were flaring into low flames, sparked by the friction from his fingers moving on her bare flesh. His hands were easing one ache but creating another deep inside her.

Her eyes closed. The pain was fading and the brandy had soothed her nerve endings. "I never blamed you for the accident, Clay," she murmured, her voice slightly slurred. "I knew it wasn't your fault."

He gazed at her face, a soft smile curving his mouth. "Well, that's something, anyway. Just for the record, it wasn't my fault I thought you were dead either." After a moment he added thoughtfully, "Maybe in a way it was my fault, because I should have known better than to believe the person who told me you were dead."

It was torture for him to touch her, to stroke his hands over her lovely flesh, but he continued to massage her leg even though he was slowly dying inside. His fingers stroked the scars left from her surgery, wishing he could have saved her from the pain she'd had to endure.

She opened her eyes and met his. He knew she was unaware of the dreamy, sensual glow in the depths of her gray eyes, making them smoky with desire. But he read their message accurately and his body responded.

He drew in a painful breath, tamping down the rush of raw desire heating his blood. He couldn't control the unmistakable flare of naked longing in his eyes, though.

Nicole saw it. "I hated you for this," she said quietly.

Shock replaced passion as her words registered. "What?"

It was a statement of complete mystification rather than a question.

"For touching me, for making love to me." Her voice was low and drowsy. "You made me come alive and then left me to die."

Clay remained still, paralyzed by her simple statement, recognizing the feeling. She had described the way he had felt when he had been told she was dead. His breathing was ragged and tortured, but before he could gather his scattered wits to speak, her eyelashes lowered and a soft little sigh escaped from her lips.

"I'm sorry about your car," she mumbled thickly. "It was such a pretty car."

He knew she was almost asleep, which was what she needed. This was not the time to go into the past. In a low, soothing voice, he began to tell her about the car he had now, giving her the details of the mileage, the upholstery, technical information she wouldn't have understood even if she were listening carefully. He heard her sigh heavily and knew she was finally asleep.

As though she were made of delicate crystal, he carefully removed the towel from her leg and pulled her nightgown down. His gaze returned to her face, and he made a silent promise to her. As long as he had breath in his body, nothing or nobody was ever going to hurt her again.

Five

Nicole felt a cool draft on her shoulders as she awakened and pulled the covers up to her neck. It was warm and toasty under the blankets and she was in no hurry to get up. Sliding toward the center of the bed, she discovered she was unable to move very far.

"Move over," she mumbled crossly.

A muffled grunt came from the other side of the bed and she felt the mattress sway under her for a few seconds.

Her eyes popped open. *Move over?*

Jerking her head around, she saw a dark head on the pillow next to hers. Clay was lying fully clothed beside her, except for his shoes. His face was half-buried in the pillow he had wrapped his arms around.

Bit by bit, pieces of the previous night came back to her, although there were some things she didn't remember. Like Clay putting her to bed.

Reaching over, she shook his shoulder several times. "Clay, wake up."

"Why?" His voice was a mere grumble.

"Because you have to get out of bed."

A muffled groan came from the depths of the pillow. "Is the bed on fire?"

"No," she answered, his grumpy tone making her smile. "The bed isn't on fire."

He slowly lifted his head, looked at her through half-open eyes, and asked, "Are you all right? Is your leg bothering you?"

"I'm fine, but you should get up. It's morning."

"You're sure you're all right?"

"Yes, I'm sure."

"Then unless you can come up with a good reason like flood, fire, or pestilence, I'm not leaving this bed. Ever."

Since she didn't immediately come up with any good reason, he plopped his head back on the pillow and shut his eyes.

Smiling and shaking her head in mild exasperation, she turned back the covers and eased her legs over the side of the bed. Some things don't change, she thought, and one of them was that Clay McMasters was not at his best early in the morning. Until the weekend they had spent together, she had thought Clay was always the dynamic, energetic, even-tempered man she had come to know over the previous weeks. He was. It just took him a while every morning to get that way.

Out of habit she moved her injured leg slowly to work out the stiffness, but to her surprise there was none this morning. Her robe was laid out across the foot of her bed and she wrapped it around her to ward off the cool morning air.

She left her bedroom and went into the kitchen to make coffee. She decided she had better check her supply of food too. It looked as though she would have a guest for breakfast. After she measured coffee and water into the coffeepot, she walked into the living room to build a fire to take the chill out of the room. Even in summer the nights were cool in the mountains, and Nicole preferred using the fireplace rather than the electric heater Jessie had provided.

On the rug in front of the fire she went through her exercises slowly and methodically. After they were completed, she rewarded herself with a cup of coffee and sat down in the rocking chair near the fire to drink it. Having Clay in her cabin, in her bed, didn't bother her as much as it should. The wall she had built to protect herself was crumbling like chalk and there wasn't a darn thing she could do about it. What she had to remember was not to expect too much from him. Then she couldn't be disappointed. Whatever his reasons were, he had made some drastic changes in his life to be near her. All she had to do was guard herself against being hurt again. That would be as easy as pushing a boulder up a hill with a toothpick. Clay had the power to make her heart sing with joy when he smiled, and could destroy her when he moved on.

She finished her coffee, then returned to the kitchen for a second cup. She also took another mug out of the cupboard and filled it with the strong brew. After adding some milk, she carried it into her bedroom.

Clay had rolled over onto his back. His shirt was wrinkled, his hair was mussed. He needed a shave and was scowling in his sleep. Nicole thought she had never seen a more beautiful sight in her life.

She set the cup down on the bedside table, then walked over to the window and pulled the curtains apart to let in the morning light, such as it was. The sun was hidden by dark gray clouds heavy with the threat of rain. When she turned away from the window, she saw that Clay was staring at her.

"Is that coffee I smell," he asked, "or is that wishful thinking?"

"It's on the table next to you."

He levered himself up into a sitting position and leaned back against the headboard. Running his fingers through his hair, he reached for the cup. After taking a healthy swallow, he rested the cup on his thigh and looked up at her. "You remembered."

"Remembered what?"

"That I take cream in my coffee." He patted the mattress beside his hip. "Come and sit down. You're too far away."

Nicole walked slowly over to the bed. Stopping beside it, she asked, "Is that better?"

"No." He took hold of her wrist and tugged, forcing her to sit down. "This is better." His eyes never left her face as he brought the cup up to his mouth again. Her silky blond hair hung in lovely disarray around her face. The robe she wore was parted slightly in front and he could see a glimpse of lace on her nightgown. She was covered from neck to wrist to ankle, and he thought she had never looked more desirable.

Finishing the coffee, he set the mug on the table. He raised one knee and laid his arm across it as he continued to watch her. "What else do you remember?"

"About what?"

"You remembered I take cream in my coffee. What else do you remember about the time we were together?"

She smiled, telling herself to keep the conversation on a light note. "I remember you need a transfusion of coffee in the morning."

He didn't smile back. "I remember everything. How your skin felt like hot satin. The soft sounds you made when I kissed you in certain places and touched you in certain ways. The way you moved under me."

"Clay . . ." Her voice was choked, husky with memories. "Don't."

When she started to rise, he reached again for her wrist to keep her on the bed. He shifted her until she was halfway across his lap, her back against his knee. His hand applied pressure behind her head to hold her still as he began to lower his head toward hers.

Suddenly in a panic, Nicole spread her hand over his chest to try to push him away, but he wouldn't let her go.

"It's only a kiss, Nikki. Trust me enough to kiss me. I won't ask for anything more."

She opened her mouth to protest and he covered her parted lips before she could speak. His tongue sought the essence of her moist mouth, his fingers delving into her silky hair. The extent of his hunger was powerful and seductive, luring her into an immediate response. A soft moan came from deep inside her and he pulled her up against him. His lips molded to hers as he deepened his assault on her mouth and her senses.

Nicole's mind spun with the devastating sensations flowing through her. How had she survived without this magic for so long? Her fingers curled in his shirt before sliding upward, her hands going around his neck. When he broke the kiss to taste and tease her neck, her cheek, her eyelids, her fingers tightened on his neck to try to bring his lips back to hers.

"I can't think of a better way to start a day than holding you," he murmured. His tongue stroked her lower lip, coaxing her lips apart. "I take that back. This is better."

The devastating impact of his demanding kiss took away her breath, and she felt as though she were drowning in sensuality. Hot, sweet memories washed over her as she gave in to the rush of passion. She didn't want to feel this gripping need for him. But, oh, Lord, she had missed this, had missed him. She felt tugged in two different directions. One was toward him and the other was away from him. Even though she was no longer fighting him, she couldn't give in completely to him. It was instinctive, a need to protect herself from being hurt again.

Clay was aware of her holding back and hated it, although he understood it. Self-preservation was stronger than passion.

He took a deep, ragged breath and loosened his hold on her, settling her back against his bent leg. His eyes were dark with unconcealed desire as he gazed at her. "It's up to you, Nikki."

She didn't need to ask what he meant. She knew. The attraction between them hadn't diminished since they'd been apart. If anything, it was stronger than ever.

"Clay, I can't pretend the accident didn't happen or that I haven't seen you in over a year."

"Have I asked you to?"

"You seem to be expecting us to continue where we left off that weekend in the cabin. I can't do that. Too much has happened."

His hand left her shoulder to trail down her arm, fingering the lapel of her robe. "I want to continue on from here. Right here. Right now. The past is behind us. We can't change it."

She reached up to stop his hand, which was edging down her lapel toward her breast. His fingers curled around her hand and brought it to rest on his thigh. "You're not making this any easier."

"I'm not going to make it easy for you to shove me out of your life. I'm going to keep reminding you of what happens between us every time we're together."

There was a hint of despair in her eyes. "I don't want an affair, Clay. I didn't want an affair before and I don't now."

His gaze was probing and intent. "What do you want?"

She could have blurted out what she wanted, but knew he wouldn't like the answer. She wanted it all, the whole package. Love, marriage, children, career, forevers.

"There's more to a relationship than sex." She tilted her head to one side. "Do you realize we rarely talked about ourselves when we were together before? We talked about your work, my work, San Francisco, just about everything but our private lives. You never talked about your family, your personal life. The only real communication we had was in bed. I need more than that."

"I discovered the same thing." He lifted her hand to his mouth and nibbled on her fingers, his eyes remaining locked on hers. "We'll get to know each other, Nikki. We have the time. Just don't expect me not to touch you. That's impossible. That's like asking me not to breathe."

"You're going to stay here . . . I mean, in your cabin, even though we don't make love?"

His smile was faint as he let go of her hand. "I haven't moved up here just to sleep with you, although I can't honestly say I wouldn't prefer staying in your cabin with you. I want you badly, Nikki. I can't hide that. I'm not even going to try. I haven't been with a woman since that weekend we spent together and my control isn't the strongest right now, but I won't try to pressure you into making love until you're ready."

She stared at him, her eyes wide and shocked. "You haven't been with another woman? Why not? I mean, if you thought I was dead . . ." At a loss, she couldn't finish.

He leaned over and touched her mouth briefly with his. "I don't want any other woman. I want only you." Taking her arms, he propelled her off the bed, then flung his legs over the side. "Now, what's your schedule for today?"

"I . . . ah, I was going to paint." Her voice was abstracted, confused.

He nodded. "You hop into the shower and I'll fix us some breakfast. Then you can paint."

"I don't usually eat breakfast."

He gently pushed her in the direction of the bathroom. "You will this morning."

Breakfast wasn't the only thing he insisted on. After she had dressed and eaten, she expected Clay to leave. He didn't. She offered to help clean up the kitchen, but he told her to go ahead and work on her painting. From her studio she could hear the sounds of running water and the clatter of dishes as he put them away, but he remained in the kitchen even after the sounds stopped.

Twenty minutes went by, then she heard the bell on the kitchen timer go off. Though she wondered what he was doing, she continued painting, determined to work. The next thing she knew he was taking the brush out of her hand and ordering her to get up and walk around.

"What?"

"You heard me. You need to exercise your leg."

He watched her walk around the cabin and set the timer again once she had settled back down in front of her easel. The whole scenario was repeated a few times more before he was satisfied she would continue on her own. He placed the timer on the table next to her with strict instructions about using it. Then he left.

At noon Clay returned. He didn't bother to knock but walked straight into the living room. He set a wicker basket down on the coffee table in front of the couch, then threw another log on the fire to ward off the chill that remained in the air. Without the sun the temperature was still cool.

It took him only a few minutes to remove the contents from the basket and arrange them on the table. He was lifting the last container out when he heard the timer go off.

Nicole had decided to go into the kitchen to find something to drink, but the sight of Clay and the array of food on the coffee table stopped her in her tracks. She noticed Clay had shaved and changed clothes. He wore a red and navy plaid wool shirt under a navy sweater. His jeans were new and fit his slim hips and long legs to perfection.

"What's all this?" she asked, gesturing at the food on the table.

"Your lunch." He held up his hand when he saw her about to protest. "I know, I know. You don't eat lunch. If you don't eat lunch the way you don't eat breakfast, I didn't bring enough food."

She joined him on the couch. "I didn't want to hurt your feelings by refusing to eat what you'd fixed."

He began piling food on a paper plate. "Sure. That's why you went back for seconds and snitched two slices of bacon off my plate."

"I'd never had scrambled eggs fixed quite that way before, with onions, green peppers, and tomatoes mixed in. It was very good." Her eyes widened as she saw how much food he was putting on each plate. "I can't eat all that!"

The overflowing plate was placed on her lap. "That's what you said this morning about the eggs."

Nicole needed both hands to lift the hard roll filled with a variety of lunch meats, onions, lettuce, and tomatoes. Once she had managed to take a bite, she exclaimed, "This is very good. I didn't realize you were such a good cook."

"Anyone can make a sandwich. Your aunt helped. By the way, we're invited to dinner tonight at her house. She said if you balk and use the excuse that you have too much work to do, I'm supposed to bribe you by telling you she made a batch of brownies from the chocolate you brought her from San Francisco. If that doesn't work, I've been ordered to throw you over my shoulder and carry you over to Jessie's."

Nicole frowned. "You and Jessie seem to be getting along very well."

He gave her a Cheshire cat grin. "Are you going to eat your pickle?"

While they waded through the abundance of food, Nicole began to probe into Clay's past by asking him about his family. His answers were virtually all statistics, with little emotion or tales of his childhood. It really wasn't much of a childhood, she realized. He had been raised by a variety of housekeepers, then later had been sent to a boarding school and a military school. College came next, then he and his college roommate, Darrell Bowers, went into business together. End of story.

When she asked what his parents were like, he said even less, giving brief physical descriptions but telling her nothing about the type of people they were. She thought that was very odd, but didn't press the issue. It was obvious he wasn't close to his parents, which was understandable, since he evidently hadn't spent much of his childhood with them. She detected a distinctive bite in his voice when he mentioned his father's wealth and extensive business interests. When she lived in San Francisco, she had passed the McMasters Building on her way to work, so she had known he was a successful businessman, but that still didn't tell her what type of man Clay's father was.

Her childhood had been so different from his, she thought as she finished her sandwich. Having an actor for a father meant traveling to a variety of places throughout the world, living out of suitcases, attending sometimes two different schools in one year. When she was sixteen she had finally gone to a boarding school in Switzerland. She was still close to her parents, even though she didn't see them as often as they would like.

"You may have noticed that Aunt Jessie has a rather strong personality," Nicole said, as she began to tidy up the remnants of their lunch. "My mother is more easygoing. Whenever Jessie visits my parents, there are invisible battle lines drawn between her and my father. Both of them love to argue and take the opportunity to fire off as many provocative remarks as they can at each other."

"It must make for some interesting family gatherings."

"It makes for *loud* family gatherings. Do you see your family often?"

"No."

She looked at him. "Why not?"

"We don't have a lot in common." Stuffing the remains of their lunch into the basket, he changed the subject. "I'd better leave so you can paint. I'll be back around six tonight. Your aunt said dinner will be at seven and we're to come for drinks first."

Nicole stood up when he did and walked him to the door. "Thanks for the lunch, Clay."

"Would it be rude of me to point out that you ate everything on your plate?"

She smiled. "Yes, it would." She paused for a moment, then added, "I never did thank you for your help last night. I seem to be thanking you a great deal today."

With his free hand he stroked the side of her face. "I want more from you than gratitude, Nicole, but right now I'll settle for a kiss."

Placing her hands on his chest, she raised herself up on her toes as his arm slipped around her waist to bring her against him. His mouth slanted over hers hungrily, possessively, then broke away all too soon.

His smile was slightly off center as he released her and opened the door. "I'll see you around six."

Nicole shut the door after he had left. Her lips still tingled from the touch of his mouth. She slowly walked back to her studio, her thoughts on the man who had just left instead of on the painting waiting to be worked on. Her resistance was crumbling like a house made of matchsticks. She heard a low rumble of thunder and thought it was appropriate under the circumstances. Lightning really did strike twice in the same place, and she was proof. She had been struck before, and burned, and was making herself vulnerable to the lightning again.

•   •   •

Nicole was still dressing when Clay arrived. She was wearing black slacks and was buttoning the front of a black silk blouse when he appeared at the doorway of her bedroom.

"Do you have something against knocking?" she asked irritably. In his dark slacks and gray sport coat worn over a white shirt, he looked as comfortable and at ease as he did in the more informal attire she'd seen him wear during the last couple of days.

Smiling teasingly, he tapped his knuckles against the doorframe. "There. Feel better?"

Blast the man! He could deflate her anger quicker than a pin stuck in a balloon. "Yes. Thank you."

"You're welcome." His gaze roamed up and down her slight figure. She was dressed entirely in black tonight, and he remembered she had worn black a number of times when he had known her before. There wasn't another woman who could get away with the stark somber color with such devastating effect as Nicole could with her light hair and porcelain skin. The dark color accentuated her beauty instead of detracting from it.

Bringing his attention back to the reason he was there, he asked, "Are you ready?"

"In a minute. I can't find my shoes. You wouldn't like to help me look for them, would you?"

His fingers gripped the doorframe. "No, I wouldn't." There was a harshness in his voice that he couldn't control. "When I come into your bedroom again, it won't be to look for a pair of shoes."

Her head jerked up, and she saw the hot embers of passion smoldering in the depths of his eyes. Tearing her gaze away, she returned to her closet to rummage around for her shoes. She needed to find them before she gave in to the temptation to invite Clay into her bedroom. The fact that she was even considering it was proof she was relinquishing even more of her defenses against him.

She finally found her shoes and slipped into them. Grabbing her coat off the bed, she walked toward Clay, who hadn't moved from her bedroom doorway. He helped her on with her coat and gripped her arm, practically dragging her out the front door in his haste to leave the intimacy of her cabin.

When she was seated in his car, he slid the key into the ignition but turned to her before he started the engine. "Will it bother you to be riding in a car with me after what happened?"

Surprised at his question, she shook her head. "The accident happened because the other driver had been drinking too much and slammed into us. It wasn't your fault."

Satisfied with her answer, he turned the key and started the car.

In a short time they were at Jessie's ranch-style house. The house was large, considering only one person lived there. Inside, though, the rooms seemed small because every one was full of an astonishing amount of furniture and plants. The decor was a combination of a Salvation Army thrift shop, a greenhouse, and a Queen Anne drawing room.

Clay couldn't help comparing Jessie's haphazard decorating style with his mother's home in

Hillsboro, south of San Francisco. Jessie's home might never make the cover of *House Beautiful*, but there was no doubt that it had been designed for comfort, not style. It was the exact opposite of the more formal, sterile atmosphere in his parents' house.

Jessie's idea of a drink before dinner was a small glass of dry sherry. Clay didn't care for it, but accepted it with good grace. Nicole also took the dainty glass politely. It wasn't her favorite drink either, but she knew it was the only thing Jessie served. Just as Nicole's mother only served a lethal fruit punch. The sherry was a close second in desirability to the fruit punch, but somewhat easier on the fillings in her teeth.

Thinking of her mother reminded Nicole that one frightening similarity between Rena and Jessie was their cooking. Maybe she should have warned Clay about her aunt's lack of culinary skills. She was used to the astounding fact that neither her mother nor her aunt could cook even the simplest of dishes. Food that was overcooked or undercooked or served in strange combinations was all the usual fare. Nicole always took small servings. Clay, however, had no prior knowledge of Aunt Jessie's cooking disasters, and Nicole watched in horror as, after they were seated at the table and Jessie had set a casserole in front of him, Clay dished out a generous amount of food on his plate.

She watched him pause after he had taken the first bite, a momentary frown appearing between his eyes. Then he continued eating, although his pace slowed considerably with each forkful.

The evening held several other surprises for Clay beyond the cuisine. As Jessie poured the coffee, she began to relate some of her experiences as a dancer in New York City many years ago. Despite the fascinating stories, his attention often strayed to Nicole, looking so remote yet so desirable on the far side of the room from him. Jessie reclaimed his attention when she began to tell him about the time she had arranged for Nicole to substitute for a friend of hers one night in a production off Broadway.

Nicole immediately rushed in to change the subject. "Clay doesn't want to hear about that, Jessie."

"Yes, I do. Go on, Jessie."

Disregarding Nicole's groan, Jessie smiled gleefully and continued. "Abe and Rena, they're Nicole's parents, dropped Nicole off here before they went to some godforsaken place in Australia to make a movie. The movie was being shot in the back of beyond and Nicole was due to have her braces off. Since there were no orthodontists in the bushlands of Australia, it was left to me to see that her braces were removed. I decided we should go to New York to an orthodontist who had done work for a friend of mine."

Clay glanced at Nicole, who gave him a smile of martyrdom. She knew this was one of Jessie's favorite anecdotes, told at the slightest encouragement. Clay provided it.

"How does Nicole get from having her braces removed to dancing in a chorus line?" he asked.

"Well, you can't have braces taken off after wearing them for two years without some sort of unveiling. A week before her appointment with the orthodontist, another young friend of mine taught Nicole one of the dance numbers she was in. When the braces were gone, Nicole put on a costume one of the wardrobe ladies had sewn up for her." Jessie leaned toward Clay. "She wouldn't have fit into my friend's costume, you see," she added sotto voce. "Not enough bosom." Jessie straightened and continued. "Nicole went on in my friend's place. She smiled her little heart out at the audience through the whole number, showing off her teeth."

Clay's eyes reflected his amusement as he redirected his gaze to Nicole. "I wish I could have seen you. How old were you?"

She gave him a rather pained smile. "I was fifteen and an idiot." Turning to her aunt, she complained, "Whenever you tell this story, you always forget to mention that your friend had made a date that night with a smarmy playboy type who said he was a prince of some country no one ever heard of. She wanted me to take her place in the last dance number so she could leave early to be with him."

"You're so practical, Nicole," Jessie said in exasperation. "You get that from your mother. Here, have a brownie." In an aside to Clay, Jessie said, "It takes a strong person to put up with practical people. You have to be firm with them."

Clay laughed. "I'll try to remember that."

Nicole wasn't sure she liked the direction the conversation had taken and decided to change the subject. "Why don't you tell Clay about how you ended up owning a country store, Aunt Jessie? It's much more interesting than how I made my debut off Broadway."

Taking the hint, Jessie passed the plate of brownies around and began to tell Clay about the elderly man she had met when she first moved to this area. He had owned half the property around there, along with the general store. They often played whist together, and although Jessie usually lost, occasionally she gave him a run for his money. When he died, he left all his property to her, claiming in his will that he had no family and that Jessie was the only person he could tolerate having around him.

Clay throughly enjoyed himself all evening and told Jessie so when it was time for them to leave. As he and Nicole headed home, he asked if everything Jessie had told them was true or if Jessie had embroidered the tales to make them more interesting.

"Oh, they're true," Nicole said. "I've heard the same stories from my mother."

"Your aunt has never married?"

"No. She said the only man she had ever considered marrying was someone she knew in New York. Unfortunately, he already had a wife. Once she found that out, she never saw him again. From several things my mother has said, I've gathered Jessie has had some rather bad experiences with men. She appears to be tough on the outside, but is very soft-hearted and generous. One of her biggest disappointments is that she never had any children."

As he parked the car in front of Nicole's cabin, Clay asked, "What about you? Do you want children?"

She didn't answer right away. There had been a

time when she had wanted children very badly, she mused. A boy with Clay's special grace and humor, and a little girl with his snapping dark eyes and glossy black hair. Those dreams had vanished like wisps of smoke after the accident.

"Maybe," she finally said. "Someday." Drops of rain began to dot the windows of his car. "I'd better go in. It's starting to rain."

Clay was tense as he held her arm and escorted her to her door. He didn't want to politely say good night and leave her, but he knew he would. Tonight she had been fairly relaxed in his company and he had Jessie to thank for that. He was making progress with Nicole, but it was too soon to rush her into bed.

After her door was unlocked, he cupped her face in his warm hands and bent to touch her lips with his. The kiss was all too brief and highly unsatisfactory when his body was aching to make love to her. He had been without her for a long time and he wasn't sure how much longer he would be able to maintain the control over his raging senses.

Nicole felt the slight trembling in Clay's hands and was aware of the tautness in him as he kissed her. He was keeping his promise, not forcing himself on her. If he only knew how her heart raced every time she even looked at him. When he touched her, her blood turned to flames.

He stepped away from her and, with his hands on her shoulders, propelled her through her doorway. "Lock your door," he said, then walked back to his car.

About an hour later Nicole finished drying her

hair after washing it. When she shut the dryer off, the silence seemed to wrap around her, and she felt lonely.

Tying her robe at her waist, she walked to her front door. She opened it, and for a moment all she heard was the rustling of the pine trees, but then she heard something else, something foreign to the usual night noises.

A faint musical sound drifted through the night air and Nicole knew immediately where it was coming from. Clay was playing one of his harmonicas.

A shawl hung on a hook by the door, and she wrapped it around herself and stepped outside. Leaning against one of the posts on her porch, she strained to hear the tune he was playing. She didn't recognize the melody, but it sounded like a lonely, sad lament. For a long time she stood on the porch and listened. From what she could hear he was very good. She imagined he was sitting on his front porch playing to the trees and night animals.

He was alone at his cabin, she mused, and she was alone in hers, both of them unable to sleep. They couldn't go on like this indefinitely. Something was going to have to give . . . and it scared her to think of what might happen if she was the one who gave in.

Finally the music stopped.

Nicole returned to her bedroom and sat down on her bed. For a fleeting moment she thought of leaving the cabin and going somewhere else, but she dismissed the thought as soon as it popped into her mind. Running away never settled anything.

If she were honest with herself, she would admit she wanted Clay to convince her he hadn't purposely rejected her. She wanted to believe him.

She flopped back on the bed and stared up at the ceiling. Heaven help her, but she wanted to believe he hadn't willingly left her over a year ago. If that made her out to be even a bigger fool than before, then that's what she was.

Memories of their first meeting came rushing back. She had been so alive, so in love. Was it wrong to want to be alive again, really alive? To love again?

Alive. That was the word to describe how she had felt the day she had met Clay. The instant she saw him she had realized she had only been existing up till then, not really living.

Looking back at that day, she realized that she had *thought* she was perfectly happy. She liked the work she was doing at the Steiner Advertising Agency, had her own apartment, she was healthy, and the sun was shining.

Munching on a fat pretzel, she stopped to listen to one of the street musicians, or buskers, as they were commonly called, play a rousing rendition of "Beer Barrel Polka" on an accordion, a set of cymbals clanging between his knees.

She had shopped for her dinner and held a bag of groceries in one arm, a fragrant loaf of freshly baked sourdough bread sticking out of the bag. Strong gusts of wind off the Bay blew her skirt around her legs, occasionally lifting it up to expose a shapely thigh before she could smooth it back down with the hand holding the pretzel. The wind yanked a lock of her hair out of the knot on top of her head and blew it around her face. Between her hair flying in her eyes, and her skirt dancing up and down her legs, she needed a free hand, so she stuck the pretzel into her mouth.

A deep male chuckle beside her made her turn her head. Her eyes locked with the most compelling eyes she had ever seen. The man's dark hair was also being tossed around by the wind, and his white teeth contrasted with his tanned skin as he grinned down at her.

"I never thought I would be jealous of the wind," he said, and gently took the pretzel out of her mouth.

His voice sent shivers of delight along her spine. Her heart beat like a mad thing in her chest as she stared up at him. Suddenly she realized she had found the other half of herself. Funny, she thought. She had never known it was missing. Until now.

Not wanting to appear any more of an idiot than she already did, she felt she should say something. Throwing her free hand up in a gesture of defeat, she smiled. "I give up. The wind wins."

"It usually does," he said with amusement, and bit into her pretzel.

She watched as he calmly munched away on her pretzel. Since she was staring at him, she didn't see the two policemen walking toward the crowd to make the busker move on. Two teenagers behind her accidentally bumped her in their rush to get out of the policemen's way, and she was knocked off balance. Her grocery bag fell out of her arm and the stranger grabbed it before it hit the ground.

He quickly finished the pretzel, then, holding the bag in one arm, took her hand and drew her away from the crowd. "Lady, this is not your day."

Nicole disagreed. Since meeting him, this was a fantastic day. "Do I get to know where we're going?" she asked as she fell in step beside him.

"Sure you do. I'm going to buy you a cup of coffee and you're going to tell me who you are and why I haven't met you before today."

"You move right along, don't you?"

"As a matter of fact, I usually don't." He sounded mystified by his own actions. "I'm making you the exception."

She went with him. There was nothing else she could do. He had said he was making an exception. And he did make her feel exceptional—from the first moment their eyes had met. The attraction had been immediate between them. Intense, natural, and excitingly sensual.

What she found even more remarkable was that he seemed to feel the same way.

But that was then. What about now?

Six

By the time Nicole had dressed the following morning, the heavily laden clouds had decided to stop fooling around with light, spasmodic showers. Large, heavy drops splattered against the window-panes with monotonous regularity.

Unable to settle down to paint, Nicole spent the morning cleaning the cabin. Her unusual restlessness needed an outlet more physically demanding than wielding a paintbrush.

She expected Clay to show up as he had yesterday and was disappointed when the morning passed without any sign of him. It was ironic that when she had finally decided to meet him halfway, he was nowhere to be seen. Her mind began to conjure up reasons why he stayed away. Some were sensible, like he was cleaning his cabin or had been called back to San Francisco on business. Some of her ideas, though, bordered on the ridiculous, like his cabin had been washed away by the rain or a mudslide.

She finally had a visitor in the late afternoon. Aunt Jessie came through the door like a ship in full sail, her yellow plastic raincoat billowing out around her, water sliding off it onto the floor.

"Grab your rain gear, Nicole. We have an errand of mercy to run."

"What are you talking about?"

"Clay came to the store this morning," Jessie said as she wiped the moisture off her face, "and bought every available bucket we had. He said his roof was leaking like a sieve. That blasted realtor had no business selling that old cabin to Clay. Alberta Dickerson would sell her own mother a broom closet without a door if she could get away with it. Why, did you know—"

"Aunt Jessie," Nicole interrupted, wrenching her aunt away from the dubious reputation of the realtor and back to the original topic of conversation. "Exactly what do you expect us to do about Clay's leaky roof?"

"We won't know until we get there, now, will we?"

"Why don't you send Mr. Bascombe over to fix the roof? It's a little more up his alley."

"Well, he can't very well fix the roof in this rain," Jessie said with exaggerated patience. "Clay may need help emptying his pails or something. The boy could be knee-deep in water by now, so get a move on." She held aloft the canvas carryall in her hand. "I brought a thermos of coffee and some sandwiches in case his stove is flooded out."

Knowing it wouldn't do any good to argue with

Jessie, Nicole put on her jacket and her red rain-coat. She had to admit she wanted to see if Clay was even there. She shoved her feet into her leather boots, which were the closest she came to appropriate footgear for the rainy weather, pulled her hood up over her head, and followed Jessie outside.

The ground was slippery underfoot. Wet leaves, moss, and mud prevented the two women from hurrying along the path to Clay's cabin. Because of the solid sheet of rain surrounding her and the necessity of watching carefully where she stepped, Nicole didn't see the long gray limousine or the silver Mercedes parked behind Clay's drenched Porsche.

The first indication she had that Clay wasn't alone was the sound of several voices when the door was opened to Jessie's knock. Expecting to see Clay, Nicole stared at the giant of a man standing in the open doorway.

"For heaven's sake, Darrell," a woman called out from behind the giant. "Shut the door."

Nicole remembered Clay telling her his business partner's name was Darrell. Clay hadn't mentioned, though, that his partner could have held his own as a defensive end for the San Francisco 49ers. Darrell's muscular frame was partially covered in a tan London Fog raincoat, the collar up, the shoulders splattered with rain. She hadn't the faintest idea who the woman in the cabin was and she didn't really want to know. All she knew was that she should never have let Jessie talk her into trotting over here.

She quickly explained to Darrell why she and Jessie were there. "My aunt was concerned about

Clay's cabin because of all this rain, so we came to see if he needed any help. We didn't know he had company." Turning quickly to Jessie, she said under her breath, "Let's get out of here."

"Who is it, Darrell?" she heard Clay ask.

Darrell grinned down at her and Jessie. "It's Little Red Riding Hood, and she brought along a friend."

"Clay McMasters," a woman snapped irritably, "you get back here."

"This is a zoo," another woman exclaimed. "An absolute zoo."

Good Lord! Nicole thought frantically. There were *two* women in Clay's cabin. She nudged her aunt and began to walk away. "Come on, Jessie. Clay seems to be surviving the leaky roof just fine."

A hand clamped down on her shoulder, effectively stopping her from taking another step. As Clay urged her into the cabin, Darrell bowed slightly from the waist, a broad grin on his face.

"I would say come in out of the rain," Clay said, "but I'll settle for just come in."

Nicole saw what he meant after she was inside. Pots, pans, pitchers, and bowls were perched on chairs, tables, boxes, and the floor to catch the steady drips descending from the ceiling. A continuous ping, plop, and plunk made her think of badly played Japanese koto music.

Clay's hand shifted from her shoulder to around her waist to guide her over to the two women huddled together under a black umbrella.

Both women were elegantly if inappropriately covered in luscious fur coats. The taller of the two women was scowling fiercely, completely spoiling the effect of her carefully applied makeup. Her dark hair hung in damp strands onto her shoulders.

The woman next to her looked somewhat more resigned to her soggy fate. In fact, she looked downright bored. She wasn't as attractive as the other woman, but Nicole thought it might be due to a lack of spirit. The first woman fairly bristled with it.

A tall, dignified man stood next to the two women with his hands stuck into his coat pockets. His manner gave Nicole the impression he would rather be anywhere but where he was at the moment. She couldn't really blame him. She was feeling the same way.

As though dripping ceilings, umbrellas, and soggy guests were the norm, Clay said, "Allow me to make introductions."

The taller of the two women looked anything but thrilled to be meeting someone. "Really, Clayton. This is hardly the time to entertain the local Welcome Wagon representatives."

Nicole slanted a quick look at Clay to see his reaction to the woman's rudeness. He didn't appear to be particularly surprised, only amused. "Nicole, this is the Bay Area task force sent to convince me I've lost my marbles. My sister, Theresa McMasters, my other sister, Barbara, and her husband, Robert Thurston."

From behind them came the sound of someone clearing his throat. Clay glanced over his shoulder and smiled broadly. "And my friend and partner, Darrell Bowers. Everyone, this is Nicole Piccolo." He gestured toward Jessie, still standing by the door. "And her aunt, Jessica Carr."

The cacophony of drops of water hitting tin pails sounded unnaturally loud as Clay's family stared at Nicole. Their reaction made Nicole wonder if she had suddenly grown an extra head. Their expressions varied from dismay to surprise to irritation.

Darrell broke the uncomfortable silence. Leaning against a wall, he asked Jessie, "Do you think it'll rain?"

Jessie chuckled. "It doesn't rain up here. This is only heavy dew."

"Do you have to make a joke about everything, Darrell?" the tall woman, Theresa, asked scathingly. "This is not funny."

"As much as I hate to disagree with you, Tess, I think this is hilarious."

"Stop calling me Tess," she snapped. Turning back to her brother, she took up where she had left off before Nicole and Jessie had arrived.

"I could understand this spurt of rebellion if you were thirteen, Clayton, but I don't see what you hope to prove at your age. Father is furious with you."

"He usually is," Clay replied laconically.

His other sister entered the fray by trying guilt. "Mother is quite distressed too. She thinks you've moved here for good and won't ever come back."

Her husband was next. His glance took in the leaky ceiling and the peeling wallpaper. "You must see how ridiculous it is for you to live here. You can't possibly expect us to believe you're serious about remaining in this dump."

Clay looked around too. "It may not look its best

at the moment," he conceded, "but it has definite possibilities."

Behind them Darrell emptied some of the smaller pails into a few larger ones. "You could convert it into an indoor swimming pool. If this rain keeps up, it may become one."

Jessie laughed and began to help Darrell, leaving the larger containers for him to empty outside. Meanwhile, Clay and his sister Theresa stared at each other, and Nicole could feel the struggle between them.

Then she stiffened as Theresa's sharp gaze shifted from Clay to her. Theresa stared significantly at Clay's arm, still possessively locked around Nicole's waist, and straightened her spine.

"Perhaps," Theresa said to Nicole, "you could use your influence with Clayton, Miss . . ."

"Piccolo," Nicole said.

"Miss Piccolo, it is vitally important for Clayton to return to San Francisco."

"Why?"

Nicole's question was apparently unexpected, and it took Theresa a few seconds to recover. "It's where he belongs. You may not be aware of how important the McMasters name is in San Francisco, Miss Piccololo, but—"

"Piccolo."

With an obvious effort on her part Theresa controlled her temper. "Whatever. Surely you can see how ridiculous it is for Clay to live here in the back of beyond like some country bumpkin. He's upsetting everyone and it has to stop. We would greatly appreciate your cooperation in this matter. Perhaps he'll listen to you."

The country bumpkin remark didn't sit well with Nicole. She hadn't the faintest idea what all this was about and said so. "Look, Tess," she said, ignoring the choked laugh coming from the giant behind her, "I don't know what you're talking about or what it has to do with me. I also don't see what Clay's moving up here has to do with *you*. The last time I looked, Clay was over twenty-one and this is a free country. I'm sure San Francisco can get along just fine if there is one less McMasters there."

Theresa had the sense to know to retreat from the battle when her side was losing. With as much dignity as she could muster she said, "Apparently it will have to. I can see we've wasted our time coming here. I can't see wasting any more."

Barbara and her husband meekly followed Theresa to the door like obedient puppies. Opening the door, Theresa looked back at Clay. "I don't know what I'll tell Father."

"You'll think of something," Clay said quietly. "Have a safe trip back to the city."

After a final glance around the cabin and its remaining occupants, Theresa clasped the umbrella firmly and went out into the rain, her silent sister and Robert trailing after her.

Nicole had expected Darrell to leave as well, but he continued trying to stay one pail ahead of the dripping roof. She also thought Clay would say something in way of explanation about his family's extraordinary visit, but he seemed to forget about them as soon as they had left.

Jessie unzipped her canvas bag and proceeded to set a thermos and a plastic container full of sandwiches onto the top of a large cardboard box. Like a top sergeant, she ordered Clay to find some paper cups, Darrell to bring several boxes over to use as chairs, and Nicole to sit down.

If they all scrunched close together around the box, they could avoid getting wet, or at least that's what Jessie thought at first. She hadn't taken into consideration Darrell's bulk taking up more room than normal, though. His back was getting wet. To solve that problem, she reached for an umbrella left by the door and handed it to him. Smiling, she glanced briefly at everyone, "Now, isn't this fun? I love picnics."

The two men looked blankly at each other, then started to laugh.

Darrell's amusement faded as quickly as a light bulb being turned off as he bit into the sandwich Jessie had handed him. Finally managing to swallow, he gasped. "What kind of sandwich is this?"

Jessie shrugged. "I'm not sure. Some of the labels had fallen off the cans." Eating mystery meat didn't seem to bother her and she calmly continued devouring her sandwich. Nicole sniffed at her sandwich—cat food, perhaps?—then she and the others slowly set their sandwiches down, exchanging appalled glances.

Jessie didn't notice, but turned to Darrell. "Have you trotted up here to persuade Clay to hightail it back to civilization too?"

"No, ma'am." Darrell took a large cup of coffee to try to get rid of the awful taste in his mouth. "I brought Maggie."

Nicole could have sworn Clay's sisters' names had been Theresa and Barbara. "Who's Maggie?"

"It's not a who. It's a what," Clay said. "Maggie is a one-megabyte computer."

Nicole was horrified. "You can't possibly bring a computer in here, Clay. It will blow up, or whatever computers do when they get wet. You've got to be joking."

"Funny, that was Darrell's exact comment when he saw the cabin. My sister was a little more eloquent, I think."

Darrell shook his head. "Tess called the place a hovel."

"So she did." Clay gazed intently at his friend. "Did you know they were coming here?"

"No, I was as surprised as you were."

Nicole had many questions to ask, but she didn't get a chance. Clay and Darrell went on to weigh the options of what to do with the computer. There were two. Leave it in the car or take it back to San Francisco. Jessie volunteered to furnish a large tent from her store, but that wouldn't eliminate the extreme dampness. Besides, the computer needed a phone hookup to tie into the computer in the San Francisco office and it would probably take more than a day for Clay's phone, which was out of order due to the rain, to be fixed.

Nicole was never quite sure whose idea it was to set up the computer in her cabin, but that's where it ended up, and Clay and Darrell along with it. Jessie, a smug smile on her face, returned to her store.

After she had cleared off a table in her living room for the computer, Nicole felt superfluous. The two men were talking a language she wasn't familiar with. Modems, disk drives, and tractor feeds were bandied about as wires were untangled and a printer was hooked up next to the terminal.

She went into the kitchen and made a pot of coffee. While it was brewing, she sliced some roast beef to make sandwiches, a lot of sandwiches. When everything was ready, she carried the tray into the living room.

"Would anyone like a sandwich?"

Clay lifted one corner of a slice of bread to examine what was underneath. Darrell cautiously did the same thing.

Nicole grinned. "They're made of roast beef, a few sliced onions, and a little mustard. They're quite good. Trust me."

Darrell picked up a sandwich. "The last woman who said trust me didn't return my car for three weeks."

"Suit yourself," Nicole said, shrugging.

She poured herself a cup of coffee and wrapped a sandwich in a napkin to take with her.

Clay looked up as she moved away. "Where are you going?"

"I thought I'd paint for a while. Or do you need that room too?" she asked, not trying to hide her irritation.

In a few strides Clay was in front of her. Darrell decided that he desperately needed something from the kitchen and left them alone. Clay's hand cupped the back of her neck, forcing her to look at him.

"Do you really mind us being here?" he asked quietly.

She sighed deeply. "I'm sorry. That was a bitchy thing to say. I don't mind you being here. It's just . . ." Somehow she couldn't find the right words to explain her feelings, mainly because she wasn't sure what they were. Finally she said, "So much has happened so fast. There's a lot I don't understand."

His fingers trailed over her throat before he dropped his hand away. "I told you before. We have all the time in the world. It's why I moved up here, to give us the time we need to straighten everything out between us."

"Your family doesn't seem to approve of what you're doing."

"Let's leave my family out of this."

Stung by his harsh tone, Nicole snapped back. "Fine. We'll do that. Maybe by the time I'm a hundred and five, I'll have it all figured out. It may take me that long. Just show me the bits and pieces of your life you want me to see, not the ones you don't want me to see. That's a terrific way to get to know each other."

She whirled around and headed for her studio. Some of the coffee spilled out of her cup, but she was too mad to notice. She slammed the door behind her with considerable force.

Swearing under his breath, Clay started toward the closed door, then stopped. What would he say to her? It wasn't the time to tell her about his father. They needed a stronger foundation between them, one that could withstand a few jolts. He never found it easy to talk about his family at the best of times. His mouth twisted into a grimace. This certainly wasn't the best of times.

"Your butterfly has claws," Darrell said quietly behind him.

Turning slowly, Clay growled, "Butt out, Darrell."

"Next you're going to say it's none of my business, but this thing between you and Nicole is affecting *our* business. The sooner you get everything straightened out, the better it will be for everyone concerned." After a short pause he asked, "Can I give you a piece of advice?"

Clay sighed and sank wearily into a chair. "Do I have a choice?"

"Not really. It's one advantage of being bigger than you."

"Go ahead. Your advice can't be any dumber than what I've been doing."

Darrell sat down in the chair opposite Clay. "You're going about this all wrong."

"Now, there's a news flash."

Ignoring Clay's sarcasm, Darrell continued. "You told Nicole something about giving her time— Don't give me that stony glare. If you didn't want me to hear what you were saying, you should have told me to take a hike. This is a very small cabin. Getting back to what I was saying . . . Why in hell would you want to waste any more time, for Pete's sake? You've already lost over a year with her. She seems to be confused and is asking for explanations. Tell her what she needs to know *now* instead of expecting her to wait until you feel the time is right."

"She doesn't believe I thought she had died in the crash. If she can't believe that, I doubt if she'll accept anything else I have to tell her."

Darrell was thoughtful for a moment. "Have you told her about your father's part in all this?"

"No."

"Don't you think you should? You want her to meet you halfway, but you're giving her only part of the map in order for her to get there."

Unable to sit still, Clay sprang to his feet and grabbed his jacket.

"Where are you going?"

"For a walk. I need to think."

Darrell didn't try to stop him even though it was raining heavily outside. Maybe the rain would pound some sense into him, he thought. Slapping his palms on his knees, he got to his feet. One down, one to go.

To fortify himself, Darrell ate two sandwiches, then poured a cup of coffee. Taking the pot and his cup, he walked over to Nicole's door and knocked.

Her expression was guarded and wary when she opened the door until she saw who it was. Darrell caught the brief flicker of disappointment in her eyes before she gave him a weak smile.

Holding up the coffeepot, he said, "I thought you might be ready for a refill. Even if you aren't, I'd like to be invited in."

She held the door open wider and stepped back. "Come on in." Glancing behind him, she saw an empty room. "Where's Clay?"

"He went for a walk."

"A walk? Now? It's raining."

"He probably doesn't even notice." He poured coffee into her cup, then set the pot down on top of a low bookcase. "You've got him pretty confused."

"I've got *him* confused?"

"Yup." Darrell bent down to look at some of her paintings stacked up against the wall. "These are very good, Nicole. Sort of like Grandma Moses's folk art." Straightening back up, he met her quizzical stare. "Do you paint in this simplistic style because that's how you would like life to be or because that's how you see life?"

"I never thought much about it. It's just the way I paint. I suppose if I had to analyze my style of painting, it would be that I paint to represent how I thought life was in the past or how I would like to think the past was."

"How would you paint the future?"

Nicole had the feeling he was no longer talking about her paintings. She began cleaning her brushes, needing something to occupy her hands. "Two weeks ago I could have answered that question. Today, I can't."

Propping his large frame on her painting stool, Darrell crossed one leg casually over the other at the ankle. "About two weeks ago Clay discovered he had a future. That was when he learned you were still alive. Up until then he was on automatic pilot, a robot, mechanically getting through each day. It was very painful to see."

He had Nicole's complete attention now. "He really thought I had been killed in the crash?"

Darrell nodded. "When I saw him several days after the crash, it was as though part of him had died with you. The part that was left he tried to drown in booze. After about the fourth night of pouring his carcass into bed to sleep it off, I decided enough was enough."

"What did you do?"

"I stole all his clothes." He smiled at her shocked expression. "Every time I tried to talk to him, he would walk away. A naked man is left with few options. He had to stay put and listen, and somehow I got through to him that life goes on. From then on he pulled himself together enough to come back to work."

"I still don't understand why he thought I had died."

Darrell hesitated for a moment and finally decided, what the heck? If you couldn't meddle in your best friend's life, then what could you meddle in? "His father told Clay you were dead when he regained consciousness in the hospital."

It was suddenly too much effort to stand. She sat down heavily on the only chair in the room. "Why would his father tell Clay such a cruel thing?"

"If you knew Hugh McMasters, you wouldn't find his lying to his own son so hard to accept. He's a man who has to run you. If he can't, he'll run over you. I don't know why he wanted to eliminate you from Clay's life, but he did it."

"And when Clay learned his father had lied to him?"

"I imagine all hell broke loose. Clay never said and I didn't ask. You may have noticed, he doesn't talk about his family."

"I noticed." She looked at Darrell long and hard. "If Clay doesn't get along with his father, why did his father send his envoy of daughters all the way up here to try to persuade Clay to return to San Francisco?"

"Who knows? I doubt if Hugh McMasters even knows. I don't try to analyze a man like him. I've never been good with mazes, and that man has more twists and turns than anyone I know."

"I still don't understand why Clay is so reticent about his family. Knowing about them is certainly better than guessing."

Darrell shrugged. "Maybe he finds his family hard to explain."

"I hope Clay appreciates what a good friend you are."

Darrell stood up. "He helped me over a few rough spots too. One of them concerned his sister. Hugh managed to convince Theresa I wasn't good enough for her and she broke our engagement."

Darrell spoke as though he were discussing the weather, but Nicole could see the pain lingering in his eyes. It still hurt. "I'm sorry."

"Don't be. Theresa had a choice to make and she made it. Her father won. Don't let him win this one, Nicole. Give Clay a chance. Finding you were alive was a shock. He's so afraid of losing you again, he's treating you like delicate crystal. It's up to you to show him you won't break under pressure."

She took a deep breath. "You've given me a lot to think about."

"You aren't going to disappear on me too, are you?" he asked with dry amusement.

Standing, she shook her head. "I'm going to get some pillows and blankets for you and Clay and go to bed. I need to sort all this out before I talk to Clay."

"Good. One drowned rat a night is all I can handle."

She reached up and rested her hand against his cheek. "You're very special, Darrell. Theresa is a damn fool."

He laughed, but Nicole could see he was touched by her gesture. "My sentiments exactly."

Later in her room Nicole went over everything Darrell had told her. She was still stunned by Darrell's revelation about how Clay had reacted to her "death." Such an extreme reaction had to mean he had cared for her then.

Did that mean he had come after her for the same reason?

There could be other reasons that he had sought her out. This time she wasn't going to assume anything automatically. She tensed when she heard the sound of her front door opening and closing. Clay had returned, but Darrell's presence prevented her from talking to him tonight. More than anything, she wanted Clay to talk to her, really talk to her. She didn't want to guess what he was thinking and feeling anymore. She needed to know.

And she would. Tomorrow.

Seven

Muffled male voices and the sound of something dropping on the floor penetrated Nicole's bedroom walls and woke her. For a few minutes she remained in bed listening to the sounds of activity coming from her kitchen. Her houseguests were obviously making themselves at home.

She flung back her covers and swung her legs over the side of the bed, annoyed to find her bad leg was stiff, and that it ached when she put her weight on it. It looked as if she were going to have to do her exercises before she faced Clay, or else she would be hobbling all over the place.

She slipped on her robe and limped to her dresser to get clean underclothes, choosing a black lace-trimmed chemise and matching panties. Excitement mixed with apprehension was knotting her stomach and she noticed her hand shook as she withdrew the flimsy garments from the drawer. So much depended on today. She could put the confrontation off until another day, but that would be the coward's way out. This being in limbo wasn't for her. She needed to know exactly where she fit into Clay's thinking, his life.

Twenty minutes later she was through with her exercises, had taken a shower, and was dressed in black slacks and a black cashmere sweater. To relieve the severity of her somber outfit, she tied a red print silk scarf loosely around her neck.

Checking her appearance one last time, she brushed a stray strand of hair back into the casual knot on top of her head. Grimacing, she saluted her reflection. You're as ready as you're ever going to be, she told herself.

She left her room and headed for the kitchen. Outside the door she took a deep breath and straightened her spine. Then, putting a smile on her face, she pushed open the door.

The kitchen was empty.

With a sense of anticlimax she slowly stepped into the kitchen. There was hot coffee still in the coffee maker and all the dishes the men had used for breakfast were in the dish rack. But where were Clay and Darrell?

Something out of place caught her eye. On the table was an empty soda pop bottle with a piece of paper folded into the shape of a flower stuck into it. Another piece of paper was propped up against the bottle. She read the bold script. "Thanks for the hospitality, but I'm returning to San Francisco where roofs don't leak. Hope to see you real soon, Darrell."

Now she knew where Darrell was, but not where Clay had gone. She took the paper flower out of the bottle and carried it with her into the living room. The computer was still where Clay and Darrell had set it up. The bedding she had given Darrell last night was neatly folded and stacked on one end of the couch. She walked over to the window and looked out. Her gaze followed the footprints in the soft ground leading from her cabin steps to the path in the woods. The path to Clay's cabin. Damn him. He had gone back to that poor excuse for a cabin.

Leaving the paper flower on the windowsill, she put on her boots and coat and went after him.

The ground was still soft from yesterday's rain and she stepped carefully along the path. The first thing she looked for when she reached Clay's cabin was his car. It was still there. Unless Clay had returned to San Francisco with Darrell, he was in the cabin.

She didn't bother knocking but opened the door. She immediately saw that Clay had begun to clean up the mess created by the rain. The pails were out of sight and some attempt had been made to mop up. The air in the room was musty and damp, even though Clay had started a fire in the fireplace. The heat from the fire helped a little, but the place was still pretty dreary. Nicole couldn't blame Clay's sisters for being appalled by his living conditions.

A slight sound from the direction of his bedroom drew her gaze away from the fire.

Clay stood in the doorway wearing only a pair of jeans, with a towel draped around his neck. As he studied her with dark, compelling eyes, he lifted a corner of the towel to his jaw to wipe off the remaining shaving cream.

"You were supposed to stay in your cabin," he said with a faint smile.

"Well, I didn't," she said crossly. "We need to talk. I can't wait any longer."

He began moving slowly toward her. "I know. I feel the same. I was getting cleaned up before I returned to your cabin." He stopped in front of her, his gaze fixed on her face. "Why couldn't you have stayed put until I came back?"

The hungry look in his eyes made it difficult for her to keep her mind on why she had come. "I didn't know if you were coming back. I need to talk to you today."

"I have a feeling my time is up," he said as though he were talking more to himself than to her. He raised his hand to cup one side of her face, his expression serious. "I didn't want to come to you unshaven and wearing clothes I'd slept in." He glanced around his cabin. "This isn't exactly what I had in mind as the place to have a lengthy discussion. I would prefer somewhere a little more comfortable."

She felt oddly threatened and exultant at the same time. Her heartbeat was suddenly thundering loudly in her ears. "We can go back to my cabin now."

"No." His hand slid over her jaw and throat to cup the back of her head. Pulling her toward him, he lowered his head to caress her lips, tasting her with his tongue. His breath was warm against her skin. "It's too late."

His arm brought her fully against his hard body, and she had to close her eyes as desire flowed through her in hot waves. "Clay," she gasped, trying to hold on to her sanity. "We need to talk."

"We will." His mouth closed over hers, and he kissed her hungrily with all the pent-up longing and frustration of the last several days.

His voice was husky with emotion when he lifted his head to look down into her eyes. "I couldn't stay in your cabin after Darrell left. I was barely able to keep from battering down your bedroom door when he was there. Once he was gone, I didn't trust myself to stay there with you only a few feet away in your bed. I knew if you came wandering out in your white robe, I couldn't have taken the sight of you with your hair tousled and that dreamy look you have in your eyes when you first wake up."

"I don't want to go on the way we have for the last couple of days, Clay. That's one of the things we need to discuss."

"How do you want things between us?" he asked tensely.

"Not the way they were before."

He looked as if she had struck him. Misunderstanding, he asked, "What do you want?"

"Honesty. Frankness. Truth. I don't need fancy restaurants or expensive weekends. I want to know what you're like deep inside. I want to see you at your worst, not only your best. When we were together before, we were in a world of our own for a brief time. It wasn't real life but a sort of make-believe. After the accident I realized I never really knew you."

He couldn't keep from grinning. "Honey, you got to know me very well the weekend before the accident."

"Physically, yes. Physically we have no problems

at all, but in every other way we're strangers. While I was in the hospital, remembering everything that we had shared, it occurred to me that if I had wanted to get in touch with you, I would have had no idea how to find you. I knew where you lived, but I didn't know the name of your business and I had never met any of your friends. I didn't even know you had sisters until I met them yesterday."

Remembering how he had had the same difficulty finding her, Clay had to agree with what she was saying. "So what do you suggest we do?"

She looked at him uncertainly. He wasn't being much help. "I suggest we get to know each other better. We talk."

"Is that it? That's *all* you want?"

Her smile was soft and sensual. "Well," she drawled. "Not entirely."

Her hands slid over his bare chest, up to his shoulders, and around his neck, bringing herself closer to his body, smiling at his sharp intake of air. There was another way to communicate besides talking.

Standing up on her tiptoes, she traced his lips with her tongue, spreading light butterfly kisses over his strong throat and jawline.

"Nicole," he groaned, his arms tightening around her as a shudder ran through him. "I don't want you to think I'm complaining, but this isn't talking."

"Well, we don't have to talk *all* the time."

"Damn, You are the most changeable woman I've ever met."

She grinned up at him. "See how it works? You just learned something new about me."

He shook his head in bemusement. "Oh, Lord, I've missed you so much. I didn't think I was ever going to be able to touch you again."

"I'm here now," she said breathlessly.

There was a tinge of regret in his voice as he murmured against her throat, "We should go back to your place."

She arched her body when his arm urged her hips against his. A soft sound escaped her lips just before he covered them in a hard, desperate kiss.

Passion flared quickly between them, strong and uncontrollable. All their misunderstandings vanished in the heat of the moment. Nothing was as important as their need for each other. There would be time later to talk. Now was the time to feel.

Clay removed the pins from her hair and combed his fingers through the soft mass to loosen the silky strands.

His hands were unsteady as he began to untie the scarf around her neck. Then he removed her sweater, his pulse accelerating madly when he saw the provocative black lace of her chemise against her pale skin.

His gaze returned to hers. "It's almost a shame to remove this."

Her hands smoothed over his warm skin, tracing his nipples with her nails. "But you will," she said softly.

Her tantalizing touch was driving him wild. "Oh, Lord. Yes."

He needed to feel her skin against his, but he didn't want to rush this. He forced himself to slow down. He had been without her for too long and he was afraid he would hurt her if he didn't take it easy.

Very gently he slid a finger under one of the thin straps of her chemise, slipping it over her shoulder and down her arm. Then he lowered the other strap, his heated gaze following the dainty silk as it slowly fell away to expose her rounded breasts. His eyes devoured and savored the lovely sight in front of him.

"I'd forgotten how incredibly beautiful you are, Nicole. My memories didn't do you justice."

His name came out as a sigh as he pressed his bare chest against her soft breasts. Her response fed his hunger and snapped what little control he had left.

"God, it's been so long," he muttered, and lifted her in his arms. He started toward his bedroom, then remembered the condition of his bed. It was soaked from the rain.

He lowered her feet to the floor in front of the fireplace, then yanked a goosedown comforter out of a cardboard box. He spread it out on the floor and knelt down, extending his hand up to her.

Without hesitation Nicole placed her hand in his. He tugged gently, and she sank down onto the comforter. Firelight glimmered over her pale naked torso, and her natural beauty left him stunned and aching.

He cupped her face and lowered his head. He had meant the kiss to be tender, but a fierce need claimed him when she parted her lips, surrender and raw passion waiting for him. Nicole didn't want tenderness. She was on fire. Fire was in her blood and a wild sweet flame was burning in her from the pleasure and pain of wanting him.

He lowered her down on the comforter as he kissed her fiercely, his tongue thrusting into her mouth again and again, his control burned away in the heat of desire.

The rest of her clothing was quickly stripped off, then he removed his deftly, never looking away from the entrancing view of her luscious body. She was so small, so delicate, so perfect. When she raised her arms to him, he felt a rush of intoxicating pleasure he had never known before.

Easing his body over hers, he couldn't resist her any longer. Moving slowly, sensually, his mind whirling wildly, he thrust into her clinging warmth. He absorbed her gasp with his mouth, his tongue moving in unison with his body.

Feeling complete at last after more than a year of loneliness, Nicole caressed his powerful body, reacquainting herself with him, reveling in the feel of him, the scent of him.

When her nails dug into his back as he drove deeper, his control shattered. He wrapped his arms around her, sliding them down to her hips, a still thinking part of his mind urging him to protect her from the hard floor.

A coiling tension began to build within him. He breathed her name and thrilled to the exquisite moans of pleasure his lovemaking wrought from her.

Primitive need reached the pinnacle of supreme pleasure as he felt her shudder beneath him. His satisfaction was fierce and possessive as he was pushed over the edge.

They returned to sanity slowly. Clay was the first to feel the cool air on his heated flesh and reached for the part of the comforter they weren't lying on to throw over them.

He eased off her, propping himself up on one elbow, and looked down into her eyes. "Are you all right?"

She smiled softly. "I feel wonderful."

His hand glided over her cooling flesh, his own smile bold and teasing. "Yes, you do."

She smoothed the damp hair back from his forehead, and her eyes were suddenly serious.

"Clay?"

"Hmmm?"

His lovemaking had given her the confidence to admit one of the things that had bothered her for so long. "I thought you didn't want to see me again after the accident because I had disappointed you when we made love."

Clay looked thunderstruck. "My Lord, Nicole. How could you ever think that?"

"I didn't know what else to think. I wasn't experienced in the art of lovemaking and you were. Then I never saw you again and there had to be a reason. That was the one I came up with."

Clay could only stare at her for a long time. Finally he said, "Nicole, the only reason I didn't see you after the accident was that I thought you had died. If the accident hadn't happened, I would never have let you out of my sight or my bed for a long time. Good Lord, woman, we burned each other up."

Suddenly he rolled onto his back and flung his arm over his eyes. Pure, raw hatred for his father flowed through him like molten lava. His father's careless manipulation of his life had hurt Nicole. "Damn him."

Clay's abrupt silence after the brief outburst made Nicole raise herself up on her elbow to look down at him. "Damn who?"

He didn't answer her.

"Dammit! Don't do this to me!" she said angrily.

He lowered his arm. "Do what?" he asked, surprise widening his eyes as he stared at her.

"Don't shut me out. I don't need to be protected like some mindless piece of porcelain. Don't treat me like some inanimate object. Talk to me."

He gazed at her without speaking, remembering what Darrell had told him. Then he took a deep breath. "When he played his power games with me, it didn't bother me, but this time he went too far. He hurt you. He hurt us."

Even though she knew who he was referring to, she wanted him to tell her. "Who?"

Lifting his hand, he brushed her hair off her cheek. After a long pause he took another deep breath and said, "My father came to the hospital after the accident. I don't know who called him. All I remember is what he said when I asked about you. And that I believed him."

She heard the regret and sadness in his voice. Darrell had told her Clay didn't like talking about his father, and that was understandable. But it was also important for him to trust her.

"Why didn't you tell me this before?" she asked. "When you first came here?"

His smile was full of self-mockery. "There are a variety of ways to manipulate people, Nicole. If I had told you immediately that my father was the one who had lied to me about your being dead, you would have been angry at him. That would be manipulating your reaction. I could have let you put all the blame on him, but I have to take part of the blame. I believed what he said. It's funny. For years I wouldn't believe a thing he said. But I believed him then. I didn't think even my father would lie about someone's death."

She leaned closer to him. "What is your father like?"

Now that he had finally begun to tell her about his father, Clay found it easier than he thought it would be. "He has to dominate everyone and everything. He has to be in control, in charge. Things have to be done his way or not at all. He's not terribly particular how he does it either. Appearances are very important to him, though. I remember one time I had fallen off the high brick wall surrounding my parents' house. When the gardener carried me into the house, my father insisted I change out of my dirty clothes before the housekeeper drove me to the hospital. I had a broken arm."

Child abuse could come in many forms other than physical violence, Nicole thought. She also realized that Clay's upbringing was responsible for the way he had treated her when they had first met. He had always been immaculately dressed and had always taken her to the best restaurants. It wasn't because he preferred expensive restaurants but because he thought it was what she expected.

"Has he always been that way?" she asked.

"As long as I can remember."

"What's your mother like?"

Staring into space, Clay took a moment to think about her question. "She follows orders. Maybe there was a time she rebelled against my father's dictatorial ways, but I never saw it. She joins charity organizations he tells her to join, gives dinner parties for his business associates, and generally does what she is told. Her opinions are my father's opinions." He turned his head to meet her gaze. "I know your aunt better than I know my own mother."

Nicole smiled. "It would be interesting to see your father in the same room with my aunt Jessie."

Clay's expression relaxed and he returned her smile. "It would be worth the price of admission."

Nicole moved closer to lay her head on his shoulder, and he put his arm around her. "Clay?"

Lord, she felt good in his arms. "What?"

"I'm glad you have the father you have."

He stiffened. "What?" He lifted her onto his chest so he could look at her. "Haven't you heard a thing I said?"

"I'm not hard of hearing. Of course I heard everything you said. That's why I said I'm glad you have the father you have."

He frowned, puzzled. "You're going to have to explain that statement."

"Because of your father, you have integrity." She leaned down and nuzzled his neck. "And honesty." She kissed his jaw and then his eyes. "And you're everything he's not." She placed her hands on his shoulders and raised herself up so that her mouth was inches from his. "Whether you realize it or not, he's made you the man you are today."

Her soft breasts were crushed against his chest and he was having great difficulty keeping his mind on what she was saying. "I'm not like my father."

"That's what I mean. You saw a devious man who controlled other people's lives and you were determined not to be like him." She smiled. "And you're not."

His hands began to move over her back and lower to press her into his hardening body. "You know me so well, do you?"

She rubbed her cheek against his. "No, but I'm learning."

And she was. He had opened up to her more than she had hoped. Not as much as she would like, but it was a start. Yet when he rolled her onto her back and his body covered hers, she forgot everything except the shattering pleasure of being in his arms again.

They had made a start along the road to communicating. They still had a long way to go, but the first step had been taken.

Eight

A few hours later Clay assisted Nicole over the uneven ground as they followed the path back to her cabin. The trail was no longer looking as unused as it had several weeks ago, but the going was still rough in spots.

They had just finished lunch when the phone rang. Darrell had arrived back in the office and needed to talk to Clay. For the next several minutes Clay listened to Darrell, then said, "Hang on a minute."

Putting his hand over the phone, he looked at Nicole. "Something has come up at the office that I have to take care of. I'm going to be tying up your phone for an hour or so. Is that okay?"

She nodded. "I should work anyway. Go ahead."

He gestured for her to come to him. When she was standing in front of him, he clasped one hand around the back of her neck and lowered her head for a brief kiss.

"Don't forget to set the timer," he said as he released her.

She smiled. "Yes, sir."

Nicole became engrossed in the painting she was working on—a still life of old books and memorabilia—and time flew by, even when she was interrupted every twenty minutes by the timer. Several hours later she was painstakingly painting the lace edging on the tablecloth, when she sensed she was no longer alone.

Lifting her brush off the canvas, she turned her head to look behind her. Clay was leaning against the wooden doorframe.

"I was waiting for the timer to go off."

She reached over and moved the dial until the bell rang, then grinned at him over her shoulder. "The timer went off. Now what?"

He reached her in several long strides and lifted her off the stool. "Now you need exercise and some dinner."

Her hands went to his shoulders and she smiled up at him. "What I need is a kiss."

Clay willingly obliged. The intimacy between them was still too new to take for granted. His mouth was as hungry and demanding as before. Shivers of delight traveled along her spine and she twined her arms around his neck to get closer.

He groaned into her mouth as she fit her lower body into the cradle of his hips. His hands slid beneath her soft sweater as his tongue mated with hers. When he finally raised his head, his breathing was ragged, the expression in his eyes blatantly sensual.

She looked up at him, unaware of the rekindled

fire in the depths of her own eyes. "Is this dinner?" she asked as he cupped her full breasts. He
relished the feel of her, her response to his touch.
"And exercise," he answered, his voice husky with
need.

When his mouth again found her parted lips he
lifted her easily in his arms and carried her into
her bedroom.

During the next several days Clay and Nicole
were inseparable. They each had their own work
to do, but the work was done in Nicole's cabin.
They took their breaks together, going for walks
in the woods, making love, fixing meals. Clay spent
the nights too. His belongings began to be trans-
ferred from his cabin to hers. A toothbrush, shaving gear, boots, clothes, were fetched when they
ventured out for fresh air or when Clay insisted
Nicole needed to exercise.

Nicole still set the timer and stopped painting
every time it rang. The simple system seemed to
work to alleviate the discomfort from cramped
muscles. Her leg had never felt better. *She* had
never felt better. If doubts filtered through her
happiness when she wondered how long Clay would
continue to stay with her, she pushed them aside.

Having Clay in her cabin seemed right and as
natural as breathing . . . sometimes. Nicole had
lived alone for a long time and occasionally found
it unsettling to have someone else around all the
time. Mostly she liked having Clay with her, but
once the newness of having him there wore off,

there were occasions when she was irritated by his constant presence.

They would literally bump into each other going from room to room, and Nicole found him to be a distraction when she should have all her attention on her work.

She kept telling herself she was being unreasonable and selfish to resent the invasion of her privacy, but she couldn't help it sometimes. She was used to eating whenever she got hungry rather than at definite mealtimes, and to setting her own hours to paint instead of having them set for her.

On the third day after she and Clay had become lovers again, Nicole was determined to finish a certain painting. A variety of interruptions and distractions kept intruding, though. The phone rang a number of times for Clay, he insisted she accompany him to his cabin when he needed to pick up some papers there, he played her stereo too loud. He came into her studio once to ask her if she had any paper he could use, then later asked if he could borrow a ruler.

As the day progressed, Nicole became quieter as she felt the pressure building inside her like a steam kettle about to boil over. The painting wasn't going as well as she hoped it would and frustration was growing in her as the hours passed without her feeling she was accomplishing anything.

Clay was puzzled by Nicole's mood, unable to figure out why she seemed so distant. There was obviously something bothering her, but since he couldn't read her mind, he hadn't a clue what it was.

He found out.

After dinner he suggested they go for a walk but Nicole declined, saying she was going to return to her painting.

"Nikki, you've been working all day. I think you should quit for today. There's always tomorrow."

"*I* think I should keep painting," she said with a bite in her tone. "If I don't keep my schedule, I'm not going to get all the paintings ready on time."

"I thought you said yesterday that your paintings were going well."

"That was yesterday," she snapped.

"Would it make so much difference if you took one evening off?"

She placed her hands on her hips. "Well, since I haven't accomplished much all day, I want to make up for the time I've lost. Right now I have a field of pumpkins that look like orange cotton balls and a couple of cows that look like goats. That's all I've managed to get done today and now I have to do it all over."

"And it can't wait until tomorrow?"

"No," she said emphatically. "It can't."

He looked at her long and hard, then asked curiously, "Is this a sample of artistic temperament, or have I missed something?"

"Don't patronize me, dammit! My paintings are important to me. It's not something to do to keep me busy while you're working. I have a lot riding on this exhibit. I haven't had a job since the accident and this is a chance to finally make some money and pay my medical expenses. I won't be able to meet the deadline for the paintings by going for a walk every ten minutes."

"Nikki," he said firmly, "I don't want you worrying about money. I'll take care of your medical expenses."

"No, you won't. They're my problems, not yours."

He stared at her for another long minute. "What's really bugging you, Nikki?" he finally asked.

"I told you. I need to work."

She started toward her studio, but he moved quickly to stop her. He grabbed her arm and turned her around.

"You can go back to your painting in a minute. First I want to know what this is all about. If it's something I've done or haven't done, you'll have to tell me. I can't make it right if I don't know what it is."

She freed her arm from his grasp and took several steps away from him. "I'm . . . not used to living with anyone, Clay. I've been alone for a long time."

He didn't say anything. He couldn't. Fear knotted in his stomach as he waited for her to tell him to go. After a long, tense silence, he asked huskily, "Do you want me to leave?"

Her answer was immediate *"No!"* Then she repeated it, this time more softly but just as firmly. "No, I don't want you to leave." She sighed and walked over to the window, looking out at the trees. "I don't know. Maybe I've got cabin fever. I feel as though the walls are closing in on me. We're practically living on top of each other and I'm having a little trouble working under these conditions."

Relief washed over him. So that was it. Coming up behind her, he lifted his hands to her shoulders, turning her around. "We'll work it out, honey. Right now we're living in pretty tight quarters, I agree." His palms framed her face, and he forced her to meet his intent gaze. "I'll try to give you more space so you can work, Nikki."

He lowered his head and took her mouth briefly but hard. "We'll work it out," he repeated. "We both have a lot of adjustments to make in our lives, but I'm willing to do whatever has to be done as long as we can be together. How about you?"

"I want to try too."

He hugged her fiercely, then released her. "Now, how about that painting?"

She nodded. "I'll just work for another hour or so, and then"—she grinned—"I'll meet you in the bedroom."

"You've got yourself a deal."

A few mornings later another problem erupted between them as they took a walk in the woods. The early morning fog had lifted, but moisture still hung on the grass and leaves. They came to a creek that was about ten feet wide. A large rotting log had fallen across it, making a natural bridge. On the other side of the creek were several wildflowers growing among some ferns and Nicole headed for the log to cross over to pick them.

Clay's hand clamped onto her arm, effectively stopping her from stepping onto the log. "Where do you think you're going?"

She looked at him in surprise. "I was going to go pick those flowers," she said, pointing across the creek.

"You stay here. I'll get them."

"Why can't I get them?"

"Because that log is covered with moss and you might slip off."

She had a sinking feeling she knew what this sudden case of chivalry was all about. "You could fall off just as easily as I could." She turned back toward the log and he stopped her again.

"Nicole!"

She whirled around. "Say it. Go ahead, say it."

"It's too dangerous. I don't want you to get hurt."

"But *you* don't mind taking the chance of falling in, do you?"

"It's not the same thing, Nicole."

She bit her lip. "No. No, it's not. You have two good legs and I don't." She glared at him, waiting for him to dispute her statement. He didn't. He continued to look down at her, his silence saying more than any words could.

"You can let go of my arm," she said at last. "I won't try to cross the log."

"Do you still want those flowers?"

"No. Somehow they've lost their appeal."

He gently cupped her face with one hand. "Whether you have two good legs or not, I still wouldn't want you to walk across that log. If you used your common sense instead of your pride, you would see I'm right."

She already knew he was right. "I hate to admit there are things I can't do," she said quietly.

"I can understand that." He brought up his

other hand to frame her face. "I care about you, Nikki. I don't want anything to happen to you. You're a very special lady." He kissed her lightly. "A bit stubborn but very special."

She sighed deeply. "I'm a little sensitive about getting special treatment because of my leg."

His hand roamed down her back and over her hip to her thigh. "And a very nice leg it is too."

Warm spirals of desire began to twist through her. "Doggone it, Clay. I'm trying to make a point here."

"So am I." He kissed her again, this time plunging his tongue into her mouth.

With a soft sigh she brought her arms up to encircle his neck. Somehow she forgot the point she was trying to make . . . and it didn't matter.

On their sixth night together, Nicole discovered something new about Clay. He came into the kitchen and found her seated at the table leafing through a cookbook. Looking over her shoulder, he read the titles of some of the recipes. "Caramel cream fudge, divinity, English toffee, chocolate clusters. Good Lord, I'm getting a cavity just reading the titles. Why are you looking at candy recipes?"

"I'm trying to find something I can make with what I have on hand. You were busy poking away at the computer and I felt like making something rich and sinful."

Amusement glittered in his eyes. "It must be the life you're leading." His lips nuzzled her neck briefly. "What have you decided on?"

"I haven't."

Reaching over her shoulder, he began turning pages of the cookbook. She batted his hand away. "I thought you had work to do."

He continued to look through the recipes. "Darrell had already done the workup on a consolidation deal and he wanted me to look at it. I've looked at it." His hand flattened on one page. "Ah-ha! There it is."

She looked down to what he was pointing at. Peanut brittle? Leaning her head back, she looked up at him. "You like peanut brittle?"

"Next to you, it's the thing I crave the most."

"Very nicely put," she muttered with a grin. "I'm glad I rate higher than peanut brittle."

"So can you make some?"

"If I have everything I need." She read the ingredients aloud. "Corn syrup, got it. Sugar, got it. Water, got it. Butter, check. Raw peanuts, oops."

Clay walked around her chair to see her face. "I don't like the sound of that. Why the oops?"

"I don't have any raw peanuts."

"What's Jessie's phone number? I'll see if she has some in the store."

"You must want peanut brittle pretty badly. What if Aunt Jessie's store doesn't run to raw peanuts?"

"Any store that sports long johns, corn plasters, and a cracker barrel is bound to have raw peanuts."

She gave him Jessie's phone number and he disappeared into the living room to call her aunt. A few minutes later he was back. Shrugging into his jacket, he said, "She'll meet me at the store. She's sure there are several bags of raw peanuts around somewhere. I'll go down to my cabin and get my car. Depending on whether or not Jessie knows where they are, I shouldn't be too long."

After he left, Nicole wondered at his eagerness at the simple prospect of making candy. During the last couple of days she had noticed Clay was no longer keeping all his thoughts and feelings hidden. He was more open about parts of his life he hadn't revealed to her before. It was as though their intimacy in bed spread out to an intimacy during the rest of their time together.

She was still bothered occasionally that they were drifting along without anything being said about the future. She didn't try to fool herself into believing they could go on like this indefinitely. Clay's business was in San Francisco. His apartment was there. He was here only temporarily and she had to remember that.

She wished she could convince herself to accept their relationship as a brief affair. People all over the world had them and survived when they were over. She would too. But she was going to have a lot of memories to look back on. She would take each day as it came, making no demands, expecting no promises. He was with her now. Somehow that had to be enough.

When he returned, he produced a large bag of peanuts in their shells. Nicole measured the water, corn syrup, and sugar into a saucepan and set it on the stove. Then she joined Clay at the table to help shell the peanuts.

"We need only two cups," she said, placing a large measuring cup between them.

As he cracked open a peanut, he asked, "Why is

it that you can cook so well and your mother and your aunt have trouble even boiling water?"

She shrugged. "It's one of life's little mysteries, I guess. Some people can and some can't." She looked up at him. "You know how to cook but I bet your father doesn't."

Clay grinned. "Somehow I can't picture my father slaving over a hot stove."

"Speaking of slaving over a hot stove, I'd better start stirring this goop." She got up and began to stir the mixture in the pan with a wooden spoon. "Does your mother like to cook?"

"I don't know. We've always had cooks."

"How about your sisters?"

"Barbara and her husband have a housekeeper and Theresa still lives at home with my parents." The two cups of peanuts were ready and he brought the large measuring cup over to Nicole. "I'll stir for a while. How do you know when it's done?"

"I'll test a drop of it in cold water, but not yet." She handed over the spoon and stepped aside. Leaning against the counter, she watched him.

"Clay, Darrell told me about his broken engagement to your sister."

He looked at her curiously. "When was this?"

"The night he was here. He came into the studio when you were out walking in the rain."

Clay returned his attention to the saucepan. "She stood up to my father for a while, but eventually he won."

He won, Nicole thought. Those were the same words Darrell had used. "You make it sound like a game."

"More of a contest than a game. He found a

husband for Barbara easily enough and had several prospects lined up for Theresa when she brought Darrell home. The only reason he wouldn't accept Darrell was that he hadn't chosen him."

"I thought arranged marriages were out of style."

"Running other people's lives has never gone out of style. Governments do it all the time."

"How can you be so calm about the way your father is?"

Turing to look at her, he smiled. "I wouldn't call it being calm. I'm just resigned." He lifted the spoon out of the thickening syrup. "How much longer do I have to stir this?"

Nicole filled a cup with cold water and took the spoon from him. She dribbled some of the syrup into the cold water and formed it into a ball. It was too soft. Handing him back the spoon, she instructed, "A little while longer."

Clay continued to stir. "Are you sure this is the way to make peanut brittle? This stuff is clear and peanut brittle is light brown."

"I'm sure." She got out a cookie sheet and spread butter over it. "Don't change the subject."

"I haven't changed the subject. I was talking about peanut brittle."

"And I was talking about your father."

"Nikki, I don't want to talk about my father. I'd rather talk about peanut brittle or the weather or"—he again lifted the spoon out of the syrup—"or this spoon. Anything but dear old Dad."

Nicole took the hint. They finished making the peanut brittle and she didn't once bring up his father again . . . although she wanted to. She found the subject of his father oddly fascinating.

She was curious about one thing especially. If Clay's father had arranged a marriage for one daughter and was working on a marriage for his other daughter, what did he have planned for his son? It certainly wasn't Nicole Piccolo.

It wasn't until after dinner that everything suddenly fell into place. "That's it!" she exclaimed.

Clay was happily munching away on a piece of peanut brittle. They were sitting on the couch in the living room in front of a cozy fire when she made her outburst.

"You're right," he said. "This is definitely peanut brittle."

"No. That's not what I'm talking about," she said impatiently. "I finally figured out why your father told you I was dead."

Clay heaved a heavy sigh. "Nicole, leave it alone."

"I can't. It's like waiting for the other shoe to drop or reading a book only to find the ending has been torn out. I can't leave it hanging. I have a theory."

"All right," he muttered, giving her all his attention. "Let's hear your theory and get it over with."

"Your father didn't approve of our relationship, did he?"

"No."

She looked at him blankly. That was blunt enough. No explanation, no embroidery, just one single word. "You wouldn't like to expand on that a little, would you? Like why he felt the need to finish me off?"

"No."

"You're not being much help. Aren't you going to say anything else?"

"No."

Nicole decided to quit while she was behind. Some instinct told her that Clay was protecting her. Knowing the reason that Clay's father had acted as he had would serve no purpose other than to satisfy her curiosity. The damage had been done. Repairing it was more important than rehashing how it had happened.

She felt Clay waiting, and let the subject drop. "What are your plans for tomorrow?" she asked.

His eyes briefly widened in surprise. Obviously it wasn't the question he had expected her to ask. "It depends on what Darrell says when I call him in the morning. Why?"

"I need to go to Boulder Creek to get a few art supplies. I thought you might like to come with me."

His hands reached for her and he urged her over to him to sit in his lap. "Why don't we make a day of it? Maybe drive to Santa Cruz to have dinner. How does that sound?"

Her arms encircled his neck. "It sounds wonderful. I hope Darrell will call early."

As if on cue, the phone on the table beside Clay rang. He automatically reached for it. After answering it, he listened for a few seconds, then said calmly, "Yes, she's here." He paused, then answered, "She's fine." Another pause. "Clay McMasters." The other person's response was loud and heated. Clay flinched and held the receiver away from his ear.

Nicole recognized the booming masculine voice and reached for the phone. "Dad, calm down," she said, but it had no effect. She let him vent his spleen for a while. Even though he was retired from performing in public, Abe Piccolo was still a forceful orator when he got going. He finally took a breath and Nicole was able to speak. "Dad, I'm fine." Her eyes met Clay's and she said firmly, "I know what I'm doing. I'll be coming up to Sausalito soon to see you and Mother. Yes, I promise."

Somewhat mollified, her father let her mother say a few words, which mostly consisted of questions about Nicole's health. Finally Nicole was able to hang up.

Both she and Clay were silent for a long time after the phone call. The outside world was beginning to seep into their isolated existence, bringing with it added problems.

Clay ran his fingers through her silky hair and met her concerned eyes as she looked up at him. "I don't blame your father for his reaction to my being here. I don't imagine I'm very high on his list of favorite people."

"He's quite protective of me. They both are."

His arms brought her closer and he spoke against her mouth. "Once they understand how things are between us, they'll come around."

As she parted her lips to accept his hard kiss, Nicole couldn't help wishing *she* understood how things were between them.

They weren't able to go to Santa Cruz the next day as they had planned. Clay had taken care of his business with Darrell early and Nicole was about to call her aunt to let her know they would be gone all day, when the phone rang.

It was Mrs. Piedmont, Aunt Jessie's clerk. She wasn't going to be able to help Jessie in the store that day due to a family emergency, which would leave Jessie completely alone.

"You know your aunt, Nicole. She says she can handle it, but today is also when some deliveries are made to the store, and since it's the third of the month, there will be more customers than usual buying groceries with their Social Security checks. I was hoping you could fill in for me today. I hate to ask you, but I don't like to leave Jessie in a bind."

"Don't worry about a thing, Mrs. Piedmont. I hope your daughter is feeling better soon. I'll go down to the store right away."

She hung up the phone and turned to Clay. "I know we planned to go to Santa Cruz, but I don't like to think of Jessie taking care of the store by herself."

Clay agreed with her. "We can go to Santa Cruz tomorrow or the next day."

She quickly changed into a pair of slacks and a sweater. When she came out of the bedroom, Clay was standing by the door with his jacket on.

"You don't have to drive me, Clay. I can take my own car."

"I'm going with you."

"Clay, you don't have to come with me. You'll be bored silly."

He opened the door. "We were going to spend the day together. We'll just spend it at your aunt's store instead of in Santa Cruz. I can tote the deliveries around just as well as you or Jessie. Come on, it'll be fun."

• • •

After an initial protest from Jessie which Clay and Nicole ignored, the work was shared among them. When the delivery trucks pulled up to the front of the store, Clay carried the crates and boxes to the storeroom, stacking them the way Jessie instructed. He helped Nicole price each item and put them on the shelves, refusing to let her carry anything remotely heavy, or climb the short ladder to put things away on the higher shelves.

He was a hit with the customers who asked him to carry their bags out to their cars. Several others asked his advice about the merits of one product over another, and he willingly gave it or honestly told them he hadn't a clue which was better. One elderly gentleman got into a discussion about the 49ers' chances to reach the Super Bowl.

Jessie and Nicole rang up sales and looked on in amusement at the way the customers vied for Clay's attention, especially the women.

When Clay had left the store to carry Mrs. Appleton's weekly supply of cider out to her car, Jessie said, "He's not at all what I expected."

"What did you expect?" Nicole asked.

"I suppose I expected an arrogant playboy. It's obvious he has money. His clothes and his car attest to that. He doesn't act like it though. When he first came in here to buy supplies, I was ready to give him the coldest shoulder this side of the Santa Cruz Mountains, but he took everything I dished out and then completely disarmed me by saying a terrible mistake had been made and he was here to correct it." She gave her niece an assessing look. "Has he corrected it?"

Nicole watched Clay through the door. He was listening patiently to Mrs. Appleton as she chatted away at him. "The mistake wasn't his."

"Has he said how long he's going to be staying?"

"No." Nicole gave her aunt a wry smile. "I haven't asked about tomorrow or the next day. I'm taking each day as it comes."

"Well, I think you can safely leave your tomorrows up to Clay. I have faith in that boy. If anyone knows what he's doing, it's Clay McMasters."

"I just wish I knew what he was going to do."

After the store closed for the day, Jessie insisted on taking them out to dinner in Boulder Creek. Since Clay's car was too small for the three of them, Jessie drove. Behind the wheel of a car, Jessie felt she was invincible and scared the liver out of her passengers as she took the twists and turns in the mountain road at breakneck speed.

Once safely at the restaurant, they had a delicious meal. Jessie complimented Clay on his popularity with the customers and he told her that any time she needed a carryout boy, to give him a call. He had thoroughly enjoyed the day, so different from his average day in San Francisco. He understood why Nicole had sought refuge in this small community, with caring people like her aunt, who would never smother her with attention, but be there when she needed them. So how would Nicole feel when he asked her to return to San Francisco with him?

• • •

Jessie dropped them off at her store so they could pick up Clay's car, and he breathed a sigh of relief as she drove away. "Where did your aunt learn to drive? LeMans?"

Nicole laughed. "Believe it or not, she's never had an accident or a traffic ticket."

"No one could catch her to give her a ticket. I dearly love your aunt, Nikki, but next time we go anywhere with her, I'm driving."

He easily said he loved her aunt, Nicole thought, but so far hadn't said anything about love to her. Maybe he never would.

Back at her cabin she hung up her jacket and started toward the kitchen. "I'll make some coffee. It will calm your nerves."

Reaching out for her, he pulled her up against him, his hands clamping her lower body to his. "I have something better for my nerves."

She gasped and clutched his shoulders as she was lifted off her feet. "Really? What would that be?"

He began to walk toward the bedroom, his eyes darkening with desire. "You."

Nine

They spent the next day in Santa Cruz. After a stop at an art supply store, they walked along the beach, wandered through various gift shops, and dined in one of the restaurants overlooking the water. It was the first time they had spent an entire day not working, and they were like two children let out of school early, carefree and enjoying their freedom.

Clay bought Nicole a small sand sculpture she admired in one of the shops, but there was another gift he gave her she treasured more. The gift of himself.

While they strolled hand in hand on the beach, he told her about some of his childhood memories of sunny days spent at beaches in California and Hawaii. During dinner he amused her with stories of his and Darrell's escapades when they were college roommates. On the long drive back to her cabin, he told her about the experiences he had

had with three different interior decorators when he first got his apartment, and how he'd finally ended up doing it himself.

She learned more about his past that day than she had known the whole time they were together before the accident.

When they returned to the cabin, Clay made soft, sweet love to her, taking both of them on a long journey of the senses, and they arrived at their destination together.

During the next couple of days Clay spent some of his time supervising the work he had suddenly decided he wanted done on his cabin on the Low Road. He had Mr. Bascombe mend the roof and make some other repairs. A painting contractor was hired from Boulder Creek, a telephone repairman arrived to fix the phone line, and a stonemason gave an estimate on the cost of replacing the loose stones in the fireplace. A new stove and refrigerator were delivered to replace the old ones.

Nicole couldn't understand why Clay was spending so much time and money on fixing up the old cabin. She didn't expect him to live permanently in the mountains when his business was in San Francisco. Nothing had been said, but she was sure doing business solely on the computer and by phone was not going to work indefinitely. He was essentially living with her now anyway, so why was he fixing up the other cabin?

Darrell continued to phone daily with reports for Clay. The computer transmitted data back and forth, but it wasn't the same as Clay actually being on hand to take on his share of the workload.

Clay knew it, Darrell knew it, and Nicole knew it. They couldn't go on like this forever.

The morning fog had cleared away early on Friday, leaving a golden day of clean air and sunshine. Nicole had gone to her aunt's store to help her straighten out her sales tax reports and Clay had left the front door open while he worked at the computer. Darrell had phoned early to talk to him about a company that would go under unless it could find additional financial support. The figures were being transmitted on the terminal for Clay to evaluate.

He stared at the terminal screen, chafing under the difficulties of working long distance. He knew he should go to San Francisco to handle the tricky financial problems for this company personally. He had arranged financing for the company before and the president of the company knew him. He wasn't being fair to Darrell, though Darrell never complained.

If only he could be sure Nicole would go back with him, he thought, he would leave today. He sighed heavily and poked a couple of keys on the keyboard. He was going to have to do something and soon.

A knock on the frame of the door had him yelling, "Come on in. The door's open."

His invitation wasn't accepted. Instead, there was another knock. He got up to see who was at the door.

"Mr. Bascombe. Come in. Is there anything wrong at the cabin?"

"No. The phone."

"Something is wrong with the phone? The repairman fixed it yesterday."

Mr. Bascombe frowned impatiently. "It keeps ringing."

With great effort Clay hid a smile. "Phones do that."

"Well, this one don't stop."

"Did any of the workmen think to answer it?"

"Yup."

Clay waited, but Mr. Bascombe didn't volunteer any further information. "Who has been trying to get a hold of me?" he asked.

"Some lady. Mac gave her this phone number here but the line was busy all the time so she called back again."

That was the longest sentence Clay had ever heard from the reticent handyman. There weren't that many people who had his phone number, he mused, which narrowed the possibilities as to who was trying to reach him. Darrell knew he was at Nicole's. Aunt Jessie wouldn't call him at his cabin for the same reason. That left his family in San Francisco. Theresa had his phone number.

"Did this woman leave a message?" he asked.

"Nope."

Feeling that Mr. Bascombe had exhausted himself verbally, Clay gave up trying to get anything from him. "I'll go to the cabin and wait for her to call back."

"No need."

Striving for patience, Clay sighed and asked, "Why?"

"She's hanging on," Mr. Bascombe said gruffly.

Clay's expression was a combination of amusement and consternation. "I'll be right there."

He returned to the computer terminal and tapped a couple of keys. The screen went blank. Then he followed Mr. Bascombe to his cabin.

Thirty minutes later Clay parked his car in front of Jessie's general store. Leaving the motor running, he hurried inside.

Nicole was working at Jessie's desk. She looked up when Clay burst into the office. "Clay! What are you doing here?"

"We have to go to San Francisco. I've packed enough clothes for you for a couple of days. If I didn't pack everything you need, we'll buy it there."

She leaned back in the chair. "Do I get to ask why I'm supposed to go to San Francisco?"

"Theresa called. My father is in the hospital. He's had a heart attack."

She sat forward abruptly. "Oh, Clay. I'm sorry. Will he be all right?'

"Theresa doesn't know. She only said he had suf-fered a heart attack and was in Intensive Care. Come on, Nicole. If we leave now, we can be there by two o'clock."

"Clay . . ." she began hesitantly, searching for the right words. "Your family needs you right now. They wouldn't want a stranger intruding at this time."

"You're coming with me," he said adamantly. "I'm not leaving without you."

"You go. I'll stay here."

He walked around the desk. "Nicole, I'm not going without you."

"Clay, think about it. Your family didn't want

you to come here and they know I'm the reason you're here. How do you think they're going to feel having me shoved down their throats? They don't need any more problems right now."

"We aren't going to be separated again. You belong with me. My family might as well get used to that now as later."

Grasping at another reason, she said, "I have my work to do."

"You told me the other day you were almost ready for the exhibition, so you can spare a couple of days away from your painting."

She tried again. "What about the workmen at your cabin?"

"I can check on the workmen," Jessie said from the doorway.

Nicole felt trapped. She glanced from Clay to her aunt and then back at Clay.

Seeing her hesitate, Clay said firmly, "Nikki, if you don't come with me, I'm not going."

"Clay," she said, trying to sound reasonable, "you have to go. Your father could be dying. He needs you now."

His eyes were serious, his voice quiet. "What about what I need? I need you with me, Nikki."

Nicole was torn between wanting to do as he asked and not wanting to intrude on his family's crisis. She looked over at her aunt, who simply nodded her head once, indicating Nicole should go.

"All right," she said, "I'll go," pushing herself out of the chair.

Clay wrote down several phone numbers for Jessie in case she needed to get in touch with them.

"We'll call you as soon as we know how long we'll have to stay. Will you call Nicole's parents and tell them we'll come to see them sometime in the next couple of days?"

Jessie nodded and gave him a hug. "Don't you worry about anything here. Stay as long as it's necessary." She reached for Nicole and kissed her cheek. "You'd better get going."

The drive to San Francisco went by fairly quickly. Clay's powerful car ate up the miles on the freeway, bringing them closer and closer to the city in record time. By the time they reached the city limits, Nicole was resigned to the meeting with Clay's family. She still didn't feel comfortable about intruding on his family at such a time. But she would just have to trust Clay to do what he thought was best.

Clay could sense Nicole's growing tension in the close confines of the car. "You look like you're preparing to meet a firing squad. You've stood up to doctors who said you'd never walk again, your parents who smothered you in pity, and me when I showed up at your door. This will be a piece of cake."

Startled, she turned to look at him. "It sounds like you've been listening to Jessie. Don't believe everything she said. I wasn't all that tough. She apparently left out the times I threw things and hated the world."

"She included that too." Along with the days and nights of pain when she began to walk again, he added silently.

"I wish I had been with you," he said solemnly.

"No, you don't," she said with a self-deprecating

laugh. "I was not exactly a good sport about the whole thing. More accurately, I was a proper little bitch. When the doctors told me I wouldn't walk again, I used every swear word I could think of and then made some up."

"Apparently the swear words did the trick. You're walking now."

Nicole kept her gaze on the road, haunted shadows in her eyes. "Yes, I'm walking now."

Clay needed to know more. "There had to be more than a few swear words involved. Tell me what happened."

"Why?"

"Because I need to know. I wasn't with you after the accident. I want to know more than Jessie told me."

"There isn't all that much to tell. When the casts were removed, the bones had healed, but there was extensive damage to the muscles in my left leg and they didn't respond to therapy. I wouldn't accept the doctors' verdict that I wouldn't walk again, so I proved they were wrong."

"How did you do that?"

"One night I asked for a bedpan and when the nurse brought it, she left one of the bed rails down. I put the bedpan on the bedside table and walked to the door." She chuckled. "The nurse about had a heart attack when she returned to find me clinging to the door. The next day the therapy changed from passive exercises to walking between bars. Eventually I had to have corrective surgery and Jessie brought me here to recuperate."

Clay knew there was a lot she wasn't saying

about the pain and depression she must have had to fight. He should have been with her to help her through her recovery, he thought, but there wasn't anything he could do about that now. There was something he could do about the future, however.

At the hospital Clay and Nicole went directly to the ICU waiting room. Nicole was surprised to see Darrell sitting beside Theresa. Clay's other sister and her husband were leafing through magazines looking thoroughly bored, and the older woman sitting ramrod straight beside them—Clay's mother, Nicole presumed—was staring ahead at nothing. Mrs. McMasters was an attractive woman. Nicole guessed that her dark hair was dyed, and it was styled to flatter her heart-shaped face. Her figure was fashionably thin and the peach-colored suit she wore complemented and conformed to the image of wife to a successful businessman.

Except for Theresa and Darrell, they all gave the impression of being separate, self-contained units. They were together, yet they really weren't.

Darrell saw them first. "Hi, guys. Glad you could make it."

Everyone looked up as Clay led Nicole over to his mother. "Nicole, this is my mother, Pamela McMasters. Mother, I want you to meet my fiancée, Nicole Piccolo."

Several mouths dropped open after his introduction, one of them Nicole's. His fiancée? she wondered. Since when?

Clay's mother looked even more pale than when they had arrived. Pulling herself together with an obvious effort, she held out her right hand. "How do you do, Miss Piccolo?"

Accepting the older woman's hand, Nicole gathered her own scattered wits about her. "I'm pleased to meet you, Mrs. McMasters. I'm sorry it's under these circumstances."

Mrs. McMasters offered a weak, polite smile in acknowledgment, then turned to her son. "The doctor asked to be paged when you arrived, Clayton. He wants to talk to you."

Clay nodded and glanced over at Darrell. "Will you see that Nicole gets a cup of coffee, Darrell?"

"You go ahead. I'll take care of Nicole."

Clay looked at Nicole. "I won't be long."

"I'll be fine."

His hand tightened on her arm briefly before he released her and left the room with his mother.

Barbara and her husband declined Darrell's invitation to go to the cafeteria, so he escorted only Theresa and Nicole to the elevator.

The cafeteria was crowded but Darrell managed to find them a table. No one was particularly hungry, so Darrell went off to get some coffee, leaving the two women alone.

Nicole knew Clay's sister was curious about her relationship with Clay. She had seen the surprise in Theresa's eyes when she had arrived with Clay, and the shock when he had introduced her as his fiancée. She couldn't blame Theresa for being shocked. It had been a shock to her, and she was supposed to be the fiancée.

Nicole opted for polite conversation. "Has there been any change in your father's condition since this morning?"

Theresa leaned back in her chair, her manner friendlier than it had been in Clay's cabin. "My father's cardiac specialist thinks the heart attack was a mild one. He's being kept in ICU as a precaution to monitor his heart. Since the doctor told us my father is already demanding to be released, it looks like he's on the way to recovery."

"That must be a relief to all of you."

"The hard part is going to be trying to make him take it easier once he leaves the hospital. His doctor said this attack was a warning and is recommending a vacation."

"You don't think your father will take his doctor's advice?"

Theresa shook her head. "My father gives advice. He doesn't take it." She paused for a moment, gazing intently at Nicole. "I would like to apologize for my behavior when I first met you. And to thank you as well."

"Thank me? What for?"

"When I saw how Clay was willing to sacrifice so much in order to be near you, it made me realize how weak I had been when it came to fighting for someone I cared about. I did a great deal of thinking after I returned to the city."

"And then called Darrell?"

Theresa smiled warmly for the first time. "Then I called Darrell. I wasn't sure he wanted anything to do with me after the way I treated him, but when I told him I wanted to see him and started to apologize for all the rotten things I had said in the past, he told me to shut up and asked me where I was. I told him and he hung up. Fifteen minutes later he was at the front door. That was two days ago."

"I'm very happy for both of you," Nicole said sincerely.

"It won't be easy. I've never rebelled against my father successfully before. You may have noticed Barbara doesn't either. She has always done exactly what she's told, like Mother. Maybe I would have continued that way, too, if I hadn't met Darrell." She smiled. "As it was, it took a trip to the mountains to make me realize I no longer wanted to be Daddy's obedient little girl."

Darrell approached their table, carrying a tray. After removing their coffee cups from the tray, he lowered his large frame onto the chair beside Theresa. "What have I missed? You both have funny smirks on your lovely faces."

Theresa smiled at him. "We were both saying how wonderful you are, darling."

He grinned. "I'm sorry I missed it." He stirred some sugar into his coffee, glancing at Nicole. "Am I to understand congratulations are in order?"

Nicole knew what he was referring to but she stalled. "About what?"

"Clay introduced you to his mother as his fiancée. Wait until I get my hands on him. He never said a word and I've talked to him every day."

"I know the feeling," she said dryly.

When they returned to the ICU waiting room, Clay's mother was sitting alone. Theresa asked her where Barbara and Robert were and was told they had left.

"You may as well go too, Theresa," Mrs. McMasters said. "Your father is out of danger. Clayton will see me home."

Theresa looked around. "Where is he?"

"He's in with his father. The doctor wants your father to rest, so it isn't necessary to wait here any longer."

Nicole stood to one side and watched the way Clay's mother managed to dismiss her daughter and blithely ignore her and Darrell. Even between mother and daughter there was none of the affection and easy familiarity Nicole was accustomed to in her family.

"Mother, Clay's car is a sports car. There isn't enough room for three people. We'll take you home."

The older woman looked momentarily confused, as if she were trying to determine who the third person could possibly be.

Nicole turned to Darrell, who was standing beside her, and murmured softly, "Have I suddenly become invisible?"

He smiled. "You get used to it."

"Have you?"

His smile faded. "Not really. It's more accurate to say I've accepted it. Mrs. McMasters isn't being intentionally rude or vague. I believe she blocks out people and situations she doesn't want to deal with. From several things Theresa has said, I gather her mother has done that with her own children. It's not surprising she does it with strangers."

Nicole brought her attention back to Clay's

mother, feeling sorry for the woman who had so much and didn't realize it.

Mrs. McMasters offered another suggestion to her daughter. "I came in the limousine. I believe I prefer to return home the same way."

"Mother," Theresa said patiently, "we sent the limo home early this morning. It will save time if we take you home rather than wait for the chauffeur to drive here from Hillsboro. Darrell's car is quite comfortable and there's plenty of room."

Mrs. McMasters didn't look at all pleased but was resigned. "We must wait for Clayton before we leave. He may have instructions from his father."

Theresa exchanged glances with Darrell and Nicole, then shrugged slightly and sat down beside her mother.

They all settled down to wait. When Clay finally came out of the ICU entrance, he immediately looked around for Nicole. He saw her seated next to a young woman and holding a small baby. Her attention was on the baby as she listened to its mother.

Clay smiled, then walked over to his mother and told her his father was resting comfortably.

"Does he wish to see me?" she asked.

"The doctor wants him to rest. He's out of any immediate danger, so you might as well go on home."

"Theresa will be seeing me home. You'll be coming out to the house, of course, Clayton."

"Not tonight, Mother. We'll come back to the hospital tomorrow around two. Dad's specialist will have the results of some tests by then." Clay turned to Darrell. "I'll be in the office around ten."

Darrell nodded. "Maybe we can all have dinner tomorrow night. You plan to stay a few days, don't you?"

"It depends. I'll let you know about dinner tomorrow."

His mother got to her feet and began to walk toward the elevator, but Clay stopped her. "Mother, wouldn't you like to say good-bye to Nicole?"

Mrs. McMasters looked up at him, a vague frown creasing her elegant brow. "Yes, of course."

Clay led her over to where Nicole was seated. Still holding the baby, Nicole stood up and briefly shook Mrs. McMasters's hand as the older woman politely said it was nice to meet her. Then, her duty done, she turned back toward the elevator.

Clay escorted his mother to the elevator and Theresa and Darrell waved good-bye to Nicole before following Mrs. McMasters into the elevator. Nicole couldn't help but notice the lack of affection between mother and son as they parted. Looking back at the whole day, Nicole realized his family didn't touch. Not only physically, but in any other way. It was all very sad.

When he came back over to her, she introduced him to the woman beside her. "Clay, this is Sarah Johnston. Her husband was injured in a construction accident."

Clay smiled and shook the woman's hand. "And who is this?" he asked as his finger lightly brushed the soft downy cheek of the small infant Nicole was holding.

"This is Tommy." Nicole looked up. "Are you ready to leave now?"

He nodded, his attention remaining on the infant in her arms for a moment.

Nicole handed the baby back to his mother, then stood and said good-bye to Mrs. Johnston. Clay took her arm and drew her toward the elevator.

"How's your father?" she asked.

The elevator doors opened. "He'll be all right."

They were alone in the elevator when the doors closed. "Good," she said, then put her hands on her hips and confronted him. "Now you can tell me why you introduced me to your mother as your fiancée."

The elevator stopped at another floor. As the doors began to open, Clay leaned over and kissed her briefly.

"Because you are," he said.

Ten

Two elderly women stepped carefully into the elevator, looking warily at the doors as though they would slam shut on them like a guillotine. Once safely inside, they smiled sweetly at Nicole and Clay and proceeded to chat merrily about their friend's gallbladder operation.

Nicole was forced to swallow her stormy words, not wanting to shock the old dears. Clay listened to the women, making the appropriate comments when they were expected, fully aware of Nicole's frustration.

When the elevator reached the ground floor, Clay calmly took Nicole's arm and kept her firmly at his side as they left the hospital.

Rush hour traffic was in full force but Clay was used to it and calmly waited for each traffic light to change. Nicole was intimidated enough by the honking horns and bumper-to-bumper traffic to hold off trying to have any kind of discussion in the car. She wanted Clay's full attention when they discussed his startling introduction to his mother.

In his apartment Clay flicked on the light and looked around the living room.

"I called the maid service this morning to send someone over to clean. It doesn't look like they made it." He picked up their suitcases and headed toward his bedroom. "Fix me a drink, will you, Nikki? You know where everything is."

Passing through the living room, Nicole saw the fine film of dust dulling the mahogany tables. The room looked unused and abandoned; the air was stale and dusty. She pulled the cord to open the drapes covering a large bay window before going to the bookcase built into one wall.

Queen Victoria looked blankly at Nicole from the silver frame on the bookshelf, and Nicole turned the picture around. Three false rows of books slid out of sight to reveal a bar complete with glasses, decanters of assorted liquors, and a small refrigerator, all compliments of the Englishman who had had the apartment before Clay bought it.

She had just finished pouring Glenfiddich Scotch over ice when Clay came out of the bedroom.

He accepted the glass from her and smiled. "Thanks," he said, pleased she had remembered how to find the bar and what he liked to drink.

As he sipped his drink, he saw the storm clouds gathering in her eyes again. "Can I sit down and finish my drink before you start in on me?" he asked.

He did look tired, Nicole thought. He had driven for three hours and had had doctors, his father, and his mother to deal with. Even though they weren't close, Clay was obviously concerned about his father's health. She could wait. "One drink and then you have some explaining to do," she said.

"You got it." He took her hand and led her over to the couch. Pulling her down beside him, he propped his feet up on the large mahogany table in front of the couch. His arm came around her, anchoring her solidly against him as he leaned back.

For the first time that day, Clay began to relax. A man could face just about any obstacle, he mused, as long as he had someone to give him peace at the end of it. He sipped his drink and tightened his hold on Nicole, loving the feel of her soft body against him. He had lost her once. He wasn't going to lose her again.

"Clay."

He lifted his glass to finish his drink and murmured, "'Hmm?"

"I think you're adopted."

He choked and coughed, finally managing to get his breath back. He shifted so he could see her face. "Why do you think that?"

"It's the only explanation I can come up with."

Her soft breasts were pressed against his chest, making it difficult for him to keep his mind on anything but how good she felt. "I have to admit I wondered about that a couple of times myself."

"Since she *is* your mother, you really shouldn't lie to her."

He smiled. He knew what Nicole was alluding to, but still asked, "Exactly when did I lie to her?"

"You know darn well when. When you introduced me as your fiancée! To most people that means we are supposed to be getting married. I don't remember being asked."

His hands stroked down her back, urging her closer. Her eyes warmed with sensual heat. "A mere technicality. I would have gotten around to it eventually." His lips found her pulse beating madly in her throat. "I've felt married to you since I met you over a year ago, but I think we should make it official. When two people love each other, they usually get married."

She gasped in surprise. She pushed on his chest so she could see his face. "Do we love each other?"

His smile was warm and gentle. "I know I love you and I think you love me." He read her chagrined expression correctly. "Not romantic enough for you?"

He leaned back into the corner of the couch, bringing her with him so she was half-laying across his chest. "I'll try to do better."

He lifted her chin with his thumb and gazed into her eyes. "I need to hear your husky laugh, to see your eyes light up whenever you see me. I need the right to protect you, to keep you safe, to take care of you. I need to reach out at night to touch you, to feel you against me during those dark, lonely hours."

His hands framed her face, his fingers weaving into her hair. "Most of all, I need to be needed. By you. I love you."

Her heart felt as though it would burst with happiness. Tears of joy shimmered in her eyes as she stared up at him. "Oh, Clay," she whispered.

His voice came to her as though from a great

distance. "I also need to know how you feel about me."

Her hands reached up to touch his face. She finally saw the vulnerability he had always kept hidden from her. He had exposed all of his feelings now and needed as much reassurance as she did.

She smiled lovingly at him. "When I first saw you over a year ago, I fell in love with you. I didn't even know your name, but I instantly knew how I felt. Even when I hated you after the accident, it was because I needed you and I thought you had left me."

He drew her against him, holding her so tightly she had difficulty breathing. Her arms went around him and they simply held each other for a long time.

Then slowly, reluctantly, Clay released her enough so he could see her face. "We still have a lot of things to work out."

"I know," she whispered.

His hands moved down over her hips, then back up her rib cage to her breasts. "But not now."

Her fingers fiddled with a button on his shirt, her eyes holding his. "No," she agreed. "Not now."

Their clothing was swept away, their passion heightening as each barrier between them was removed. Each stroke of a hand, each intimate kiss, was a promise, bringing them closer to the final pleasure.

When they were naked, bodies pressed tight together, Clay's hands moved quickly, almost frantically, over her, yet he took her mouth slowly, his lips and tongue blatantly sensual. The contrast had her writhing beneath him, arching her hips into his, searching for an end to the sweet agony deep inside her.

Knowing they were loved broke all restraints as their burning desire caught up with their searing need. Clay's tongue plunged into her mouth the same time his hard body entered her intimate heat.

Their bodies fused together, renewing the commitment their hearts had already made. As he thrust his hips against hers, Clay looked down at her closed eyes, hearing the soft, melting sounds in her throat.

"Nikki," he murmured hoarsely. "Look at me."

Slowly she opened her eyes.

Continuing to move against her, he said raggedly, "I love you."

She met his hot gaze and whispered achingly, "I love you."

With a final thrust the world splintered and shattered around them.

It was a long time before either of them felt like moving. Lifting his weight partially off her but staying deep inside her, Clay gazed down at her.

"Nikki, will you marry me?"

She smiled. "I thought you'd never ask."

"Oh, Nikki," he said against her lips. "I'll make you happy."

"You already have, Clay. I can't imagine being any happier than I am right now."

He kissed her lingeringly. "I'll take that as a challenge. I plan to make you the happiest woman in the world."

Her arms around his neck brought his head

back down so she could kiss him. "Does that include feeding me? I'm starving."

Laughing, he eased off her and stood beside the couch, extending his hand to her. "I'll see what I can do."

While Nicole showered, Clay called a deli and ordered a variety of sandwiches and salads to be delivered. There was nothing to eat in his apartment since he had gone to the cabin. Tomorrow they would have to buy some groceries if they were going to stay for a few days. Especially coffee.

Wrapped in a towel, Nicole searched through the suitcase Clay had packed for her. She didn't realize she was smiling until he spoke from the doorway.

"What's so funny?"

Indicating the open suitcase, she said, "You have an odd idea of what a woman needs to pack. You left out my nightgown and robe."

He walked toward her. "You haven't needed a nigthgown lately, and I have several robes here." He slid open his closet door and took out a white robe. Standing in front of her, he held it out for her to put on. As soon as her arms were in the sleeves, he loosened the towel from around her, letting it drop to the floor as his hands glided over her fragrant flesh.

She leaned against him and sighed, tilting her head back to meet his warm mouth. His arms slid around her under the robe and he took her mouth, her name on his lips before he kissed her.

He would never get enough of her, he thought as he lifted his head. "I have something else for you to put on. Then you'll be fully dressed."

He walked over to a tall dresser and opened the top drawer. Coming back to her, he lifted her hand and placed a small white velvet box in her palm.

Nicole lifted the hinged lid and gasped. Tucked into the box was a stunning emerald stone surrounded by diamonds in an antique silver setting.

"Oh, Clay. It's beautiful."

He took the ring out and placed it on her finger. "I bought it over a year ago. I was going to give it to you when we returned from our first weekend together." He lifted her hand to his mouth, his eyes never leaving hers. "There's a matching silver band that goes with it. I don't want to wait too long to put it next to this ring."

Just then the doorbell rang. Clay gathered the front of the robe together and tied the sash at her waist, concealing her tempting body. He smiled down at her, then went to answer the door.

During the next few days Clay spent his mornings at his office, catching up on his work. In the afternoons he picked Nicole up at his apartment before going to the hospital. She never went in with him to see his father, but he wanted her to go with him just the same.

One morning Nicole went shopping, stocking the apartment with food and buying the clothes she needed for her stay in San Francisco. One evening they had dinner with Darrell and Theresa, and the next evening they drove to Sausalito to see her parents.

Abe and Rena Piccolo were cautiously polite at first with Clay. Jessie had paved the way by phoning her sister to tell her Nicole would be bringing

Clay with her. Even though Jessie was obviously pleased Clay and Nicole were together again, Rena and Abe reserved their judgment.

Gradually, as the evening progressed and they saw how Clay looked at their daughter, and saw the ring he had given her, they lost their prior prejudice against him. They eventually asked where he and Nicole planned to live, and Nicole told them they would be living at the cabin until she finished her paintings for the exhibition.

"Nicole paints well there," Clay explained, "and it wouldn't be fair to make her move right now. Later we'll be staying in my apartment and we'll keep the cabin as a weekend retreat. One of the bedrooms can be converted into a studio for her until we have time to find a bigger place to live."

When the subject of the wedding came up, Rena immediately had some suggestions. As she warmed to the subject, the plans became more elaborate, from a wedding in a vineyard to a ceremony on the *QE* II. Nicole tried to apply a brake to the runaway plans, but her mother was having so much fun, she gave up.

As Rena chattered, Nicole saw Clay's expression turn pensive, and she wondered what he was thinking. So much had happened so fast the last couple of days, they hadn't had time to discuss any definite wedding plans.

On the drive back to his apartment, she brought up the subject of his cabin. He hadn't mentioned yet what he planned to do with it.

"Clay, why are you spending so much money fixing up your cabin if you don't plan on living there?"

"The cabin has served its purpose, but I have some rather fond memories of it, leaky roof and all." He slanted a quick look at her as they exited from the Waldo Tunnel heading toward the Golden Gate Bridge. "I thought we would give it to Darrell and Theresa for a wedding present. If he hadn't agreed to take over the business so I could be near you, it would have been difficult to work everything out between us."

"Do you think your sister will want to stay in the cottage? She wasn't terribly impressed with it the first time she saw it."

"Once it's no longer a hovel, she'll like it. She's lived a pretty sheltered life. It will do her good to rough it once in a while."

When they reached his apartment, Clay shut off the engine but didn't immediately get out of the car. Nicole looked at him, surprised to see him frowning with his fingers tapping the wheel.

"Clay? What's wrong?"

He turned his head to meet her puzzled gaze. "My father asked to see you."

For a moment Nicole let his words soak in. Earlier he had mentioned his father had been moved to a private room and would soon be released, but he hadn't said he had talked to his father about her.

"Your father *asked* to see me?"

"As I was leaving his room this afternoon. He suggested tomorrow. I told him it was up to you."

She smiled. "Do you think he's going to try to buy me off? Killing me didn't seem to work."

Clay didn't smile back. "You don't have to go, Nikki."

She shrugged. "I would like to meet him. I'm going to have to someday. It might as well be tomorrow."

"Are you sure?"

She put her hand over his as he gripped the steering wheel. "Clay, we have to meet sometime. I'll tell you what. You stand outside the door and if he comes at me with a bedpan, I'll yell for help."

This time he smiled.

Much later Nicole lay in Clay's arms, fully aware of Clay staring up at the ceiling rather than sleeping.

"Clay?"

His arm tightened around her when he realized she was still awake. "What?"

"Something's bothering you other than my visit to your father. I wish you would tell me. I would rather know what it is than try to guess."

His hand smoothed over her back. "I was thinking about all the plans your mother was making for our wedding."

"She gets carried away sometimes. We don't have to go along with her ideas. She'll understand if we don't agree with her."

"One thing she won't understand is my parents not attending the wedding. There's a chance that could happen." He rolled her over onto her back and gazed down at her. "I don't want to start our marriage with bad feelings between our families. If my father refuses to come to our wedding . . ."

"He'll come," she insisted. "If only to keep up appearances. Even if he doesn't, our wedding is between you and me. Our marriage already exists."

The tension left him and she felt his smile

against her mouth as he lowered his head and kissed her. "I don't want you to be disappointed, that's all," he said. "A woman's wedding is important to her. It's supposed to be a special day in a woman's life."

She caressed his cheek. "It will be special," she said softly. "You'll be there."

Clay pulled her under him and kissed her deeply, hungrily, his concerns evaporating. She was right. As long as they were together, nothing else mattered. The world was an imperfect place with imperfect people. The only thing that mattered was being together.

Nicole knew she had sounded carefree about meeting Clay's father, but she certainly didn't feel like making jokes when she was in the elevator on her way up to Mr. McMasters's room. She had taken special pains with her appearance, had bought a new dress that morning, and spent longer than usual on her hair and makeup. She kept telling herself not to be nervous, but it didn't help. She was petrified. It wasn't every day she met a man who had pronounced her dead.

Clay stopped outside his father's room and put his hand on her arm. "I'll be right here."

She gave him a rather feeble smile and pushed open the door.

Clay's father was sitting in a chair looking out the window. Wearing a navy blue dressing gown over light blue pajamas, he looked a little pale but otherwise seemed a healthy, vital man. He had to

know she was in the room but he didn't acknowl-
edge her presence.

So that's how it was going to be, she thought.

She walked over to the other chair several feet
away from him and sat down. Crossing one leg
over the other, she placed her purse in her lap
and laid her hands on top of it. If he expected her
to make the first move, he had a long wait.

Finally Hugh McMasters turned his head to look
at her. He didn't speak and she calmly stared
back at him.

When he realized she wasn't easily intimidated,
he grudgingly spoke. "Well?"

"Well, what?"

"Have you nothing to say?"

"You asked to see me, Mr. McMasters. Apparently you have something to say to me."

His expression changed slightly. "I thought perhaps we should meet. Clayton has indicated he is
seriously involved with you. Is that true?"

"You obviously don't believe Clay. Why would
you believe me?"

Hugh looked thoughtful as he glared at her long
and hard. "It appears I've underestimated you,
Miss Piccolo."

"You make it sound as though we're enemies,
Mr. McMasters, weighing my strengths against
yours. I have no animosity toward you, even though
you told Clay I was dead."

"Are you expecting me to apologize?"

"No."

"It's just as well, because I won't apologize for
doing what I thought was best for my son."

"What about what Clay thinks is best for him,

Mr. McMasters? Doesn't he have any say in his own life?"

"Children don't always know what is best for them, Miss Piccolo. Perhaps when you are a parent, you will understand that."

"When I have children, Mr. McMasters, they will be your grandchildren."

He looked startled but quickly covered it with a scowl. "I don't approve."

She couldn't help smiling. "I didn't think you would."

He gave her an assessing look. "You aren't afraid of me, are you?"

"I'd like to tell you a little story, Mr. McMasters. It's about a dog that belonged to our gardener when we lived in England. He growled and snarled at anyone who came near him. He was tied to a rope that let him go only so far, so one day I sat down just beyond the reach of that rope. I sat there for quite a while as he barked and bared his teeth. It was the only way he knew how to treat people.

"When he realized he couldn't make me go away, he sat back and growled at me occasionally. My reaction mystified him. Eventually he laid down with his head between his paws and stared at me.

"When I held out my hand, he looked as if he wanted to bite it, but he only sniffed it and then sat back.

"You remind me of that dog, Mr. McMasters. Snapping and barking at everyone around you, testing those who want to get close to you, and becoming even more ferocious when you scare them away. You don't want to scare them away, but you don't know any other way to treat them."

Hugh McMasters looked thunderstruck. In a hoarse voice he said, "You're an impertinent woman, Miss Piccolo."

"Yes, sir. I suppose from your viewpoint, I am. I don't scare easily, Mr. McMasters. I love your son and he loves me. Clay doesn't need your approval, but he would like your blessing."

Clay's father looked at her with an odd expression. After a long tense silence, he bellowed, "Clayton!"

The door opened immediately. Clay rushed into the room, then stopped abruptly. He looked at Nicole, who was sitting in her chair, smiling serenely at him. Then he looked at his father. *Good Lord,* he thought in astonishment. *He's smiling. At Nicole.*

"Clayton," his father said, "I hope you know what you're doing. This woman is going to give you a run for your money. My grandchildren will undoubtedly be as headstrong and stubborn as she is. For what it's worth, I wish you both a long and healthy life."

Clay stared at his father as though he had just lost his mind and Clay hadn't the faintest idea where he was going to look for it.

Nicole looked up at Clay. "Clayton, darling. Your mouth is open."

Hugh McMasters began to laugh. It was a rather rusty sound, but it was definitely a laugh.

Later that evening Nicole was sitting on the bed

Indian-style as she brushed her hair. Clay came out of the bathroom, a towel draped around his hips. He sat down on the bed behind her and took the brush out of her hand.

With gentle strokes he continued to brush her hair, loving the silky feel of it. The ends were still damp from her shower. His free hand lifted to weave through her hair, massaging her neck and shoulder.

She leaned back against him. "Hmm. That feels good."

"You're a silver-haired witch, Nikki. Casting your spell over everyone around you. You're not going to tell me what happened between you and my father, are you?"

Turning around, she pressed him back on the bed, landing on top of him. The tie came loose on her robe and her breasts were crushed against his chest.

"Witches don't give away their secrets."

His hands went under her robe to find her bare flesh, moving over her, pressing her into his aroused body. "You keep your secrets, honey. I don't mind being under your spell. In fact, I will gladly sign on for a lifetime of your magic."

She smiled down at him, her soft hands sliding over his chest and waist. Then she slowly raised her hips so she could loosen his towel.

"A lifetime," she breathed against his mouth. "I hope it's long enough."

Three months later Nicole was getting ready for their first dinner party. Earlier she had set the table with the china they had received as a wedding present from her parents and the fine crystal given to them by Clay's parents. Everything was ready to serve once their guests arrived.

In their bedroom Clay took his dinner jacket off a hanger and shrugged into it. As he turned, he watched his wife fasten a string of pearls around her slender neck. Dressed in a slim black evening gown, her silvery hair piled on top of her head, she looked regally exotic and his body tightened.

He came over to stand behind her, watching her reflection in the mirror. "You're very beautiful, Mrs. McMasters."

Meeting his eyes in the mirror, she smiled. "Thank you. You look fairly devastating yourself."

"Are you sure this dinner party is such a good idea?"

"It's a little late to change our minds, darling. Your mother phoned to say they were coming, Aunt Jessie has driven up from the mountains, Darrell and Theresa and my parents will be here any minute." She smiled. "We have a lot to celebrate. My exhibit was sold out and we have an announcement to make. What better reason for our first dinner party?"

His hand moved around her waist and over her stomach. "I'd rather have you two all to myself."

She placed her hand over his, pressing his palm against the small life growing inside her. A warm glow flowed through her and she wanted to share her happiness with the world, but would settle for sharing it with their families.

She gazed at Clay in the mirror, a soft, loving smile curving her mouth and warming her eyes.

They had traveled down two separate roads for a long time, but now they were going to journey down the same road forever, adding a few little McMasterses along the way.

Clay turned her around and lowered his head. The doorbell rang as he was kissing her and he raised his head, smiling at her.

"Lets get this over with. I want to be alone with my family."

THE EDITOR'S CORNER

One of the best "presents" I've received at Bantam is the help of the very talented and wonderfully enthusiastic Barbara Alpert, who has written the copy for the back cover of almost every LOVESWEPT romance since the first book. (In fact, only three in all this time haven't been written by Barbara, and I wrote those.) As usual, Barbara has done a superb job of showcasing all the books next month, and so I thought I would give you a sneak peek at her copy on the marvelous books you can expect to keep your holiday spirits high.

First, we are delighted to welcome a brand-new writer—and our first Canadian author—Judy Gill, with **HEAD OVER HEELS,** LOVESWEPT #228. "The sultry laughter and tantalizing aromas that wafted across the fence from next door were enough to make a grown man cry, Buck Halloran thought—or else climb eight-foot fences! But the renowned mountain climber was confined to a wheelchair, casts on one arm and one leg . . . how could he meet the woman behind the smoky voice, the temptress who was keeper of the goodies? . . . He had to touch her, searing her lips with kisses that seduced her heart and soul—and Darcy Gallagher surrendered to the potent magic of his embrace. But the handsome wanderer who whispered sexy promises to her across the hedge at midnight had his eyes on a higher mountain, a new adventure, while she yearned to make a home for children and the man she loved. Could they join their lives and somehow share the dreams that gave them joy?"

Sandra Brown has given us a memorable gift of love in **TIDINGS OF GREAT JOY,** LOVESWEPT #229. As Barbara describes it, "Ria Lavender hadn't planned on spending a passionate Christmas night in front of a roaring fire with Taylor Mackensie. But somehow the scents of pine tree, wood smoke, and male flesh produced a kind of spontaneous combustion inside her, and morning found the lovely architect lying on her silver fox coat beside the mayor-elect, a man she hardly knew. Ten weeks later she knew she was pregnant with Taylor's child . . . and insisted they had to marry. A marriage 'in name only,' she promised him. Taylor agreed to a wedding, but shocked Ria with his demand that they live together as husband and wife—in every way. She couldn't deny she wanted him, the lady-killer with the devil's grin, but

(continued)

there was danger in succumbing to the heat he roused—in falling for a man she couldn't keep."

Prepare yourself for a session of hearty laughter and richly warming emotion when you read Joan Elliott Pickart's **ILLUSIONS**, LOVESWEPT #230. Barbara teases you unmercifully with her summary of this one! "There was definitely a naked man asleep in Cassidy Cole's bathtub! With his ruggedly handsome face and 'kissin' lips,' Sagan Jones was a single woman's dream, and how could she resist a smooth-talking vagabond with roving hands who promised he'd stay only until his luggage caught up with him? Sagan had come to Cherokee, Arizona, after promising Cassidy's brother he'd check up on her. He'd flexed his muscles, smiled his heart-stopping smile, and won over everyone in town except her. . . . Sagan had spent years running from loneliness, and though his lips vowed endless pleasures, Cassidy knew he wasn't a man to put down roots. . . . Could she make him see that in a world full of mirages and dreams that died with day, her love was real and everlasting?"

Hagen strikes again in Kay Hooper's delightful **THE FALL OF LUCAS KENDRICK**, LOVESWEPT #231. As Barbara tells you, "Time was supposed to obscure memories, but when Kyle Griffon saw the sunlight glinting off Lucas Kendrick's hair, she knew she'd never stopped waiting for him. Ten years before, he'd awakened her woman's passion, and when he left without a word, her quicksilver laughter had turned to anger, and her rebel's heart to a wild flirtation with danger—anything to forget the pain of losing him. Now he was back, and he needed her help in a desperate plan— but did she dare revive the flame of desire that once had burned her?" Only Josh, Raven, Rafferty, a few other fictional characters, Kay, Barbara, and I know right now. Be sure that you're one of the first next month to get the answer!

You can have the wish you wish as you read this: another great love story from Iris Johansen who gives you **STAR LIGHT, STAR BRIGHT**, LOVESWEPT #232. "When the golden-haired rogue in the black leather jacket dodged a barrage of bullets to rescue her, Quenby Swenson thrilled . . . with fear and with excitement," says Barbara most accurately. "Gunner Nilsen had risked his life to save her, but when he promised to cherish her for a lifetime, she refused to believe him. And yet she knew somehow he'd

(continued)

never lie to her, never hurt her, never leave her—even though she hardly knew him at all. He shattered her serenity, rippled her waters, vowing to play her body like the strings of a harp . . . until he'd learned all the melodies inside her. Quenby felt her heart swell with yearning for the dreams Gunner wove with words and caresses. Did she dare surrender to this mysterious man of danger, the untamed lover who promised her their souls were entwined for all time?"

For one of the most original, whimsical, and moving romances ever, you can't beat **THE BARON,** LOVESWEPT #233 by Sally Goldenbaum. Barbara whets your appetite with this terrific description: "Disguised as a glittering contessa for a glamorous mystery weekend, Hallie Finnegan knew anything was possible—even being swept into the arms of a dashing baron! She'd never been intriguing before, never enchanted a worldly man who stunned her senses with hungry kisses beneath a full moon. Once the 'let's pretend mystery' was solved, though, they shed their costumes, revealing Hallie for the shy librarian with freckles she was— but wealthy, elegant Nick Harrington was still the baron . . . and not in her league. When Nick turned up on her doorstep in pursuit of his fantasy lady, Hallie was sure he'd discover his mistake and run for the hills!"

It's a joy for me to send you the same heartfelt wishes for the season that we've sent you every year since LOVE-SWEPT began. May your New Year be filled with all the best things in life—the company of good friends and family, peace and prosperity, and of course, love.

Warm wishes for 1988 from all of us at LOVESWEPT.

Sincerely,

Carolyn Nichols

Carolyn Nichols
   Editor

LOVESWEPT
Bantam Books, Inc.
666 Fifth Avenue
New York, NY 10103

HANDSOME, SPACE-SAVER
BOOKRACK

Nevco US Pat. 3,464,565

ONLY
$9.95

- hand-rubbed walnut finish
- patented sturdy construction
- assembles in seconds
- assembled size 16" x 8"

Perfect as a desk or table top library— Holds both hardcovers and paperbacks.

- -

LOVESWEPT

Love Stories you'll never forget by authors you'll always remember

☐	21795	**Where The Heart Is #174** Eugenia Riley	$2.50
☐	21796	**Expose #175** Kimberli Wagner	$2.50
☐	21794	**'Til The End Of Time #176** Iris Johansen	$2.50
☐	21802	**Hard Habit To Break #177** Linda Cajio	$2.50
☐	21807	**Disturbing The Peace #178** Peggy Webb	$2.50
☐	21801	**Kaleidoscope #179** Joan Elliott Pickart	$2.50
☐	21797	**The Dragon Slayer #180** Patt Bucheister	$2.50
☐	21790	**Robin And Her Merry People #181** Fayrene Preston	$2.50
☐	21756	**Makin' Whoopee #182** Billie Green	$2.50
☐	21811	**Tangles #183** Barbara Boswell	$2.50
☐	21812	**Sultry Nights #184** Anne Kolaczyk & Ed Kolaczyk	$2.50
☐	21809	**Sunny Chandler's Return #185**	$2.50
☐	21810	**Fiddlin' Fool #186** Susan Richardson	$2.50
☐	21814	**Last Bridge Home #187** Iris Johansen	$2.50
☐	21822	**Detour To Euphoria #188** Becky Lee Weyrich	$2.50
☐	21798	**In Serena's Web #189** Kay Hooper	$2.50
☐	21823	**Wild Poppies #190** Joan Elliott Pickart	$2.50
☐	21828	**Across the River of Yesterday #191** Iris Johansen	$2.50
☐	21813	**The Joy Bus #192** Peggy Webb	$2.50
☐	21824	**Raven On the Wing #193** Kay Hooper	$2.50
☐	21829	**Not A Marrying Man #194** Barbara Boswell	$2.50
☐	21825	**Wind Warning #195** Sara Orwig	$2.50
☐	21771	**Solid Gold Prospect #196** Hertha Schulze	$2.50

Prices and availability subject to change without notice.

Buy them at your local bookstore or use this handy coupon for ordering:

Bantam Books, Inc., Dept. SW3, 414 East Golf Road, Des Plaines, Ill. 60016

Please send me the books I have checked above. I am enclosing $_____
(please add $1.50 to cover postage and handling). Send check or money order
—no cash or C.O.D.s please.

Mr/Ms_____

Address_____

City_____ State/Zip_____

SW3—8/87

Please allow four to six weeks for delivery. This offer expires 2/88.